Between A Rock
And a Bad Place

James Manning

Copyright © 2012 Author Name

All rights reserved.

ISBN: 9781521466001

DEDICATION

For my family, you know who you are.

Also for Paul Walker, a legend who inspired me, and in part, this tale

ACKNOWLEDGMENTS

Thanks go out to Chris, Liam, Lauren, and the riding stables that let me use their yard for the cover.

1

The sun was low over the gentle hills of England's historic Midlands. For centuries, the small central county of Warwickshire was known for Shakespeare, castles and canals. However, nestled deep in the green and pleasant land the small market town of Lower Hampton dozed comfortably in the evening cool. The old town hall, the crooked and listing houses, some with Tudor wood beams black on white, were over 400 years old, dating back to the 1600's. A large cobbled market square sat in the centre of the crossroads like a hunting rifle's scope. The town was home to over 30,000 largely honest, hardworking citizens.

Over the hills, where the town lay spread out picturesquely, twisty, winding country lanes followed high hedges like river of tarmac, leading walkers, horse riders and tourists to the local attractions and scattering of small farms, homes and hamlets. Although never in any tourist guidebooks, or internet recommended sites Lower Hampton had a charm of which only the English countryside could boast, almost a place frozen in time.

The horizon glowed as the spring sun sank behind the tree-lined skyline. From a hillside vantage point, the streetlights of the town, the ugly dual carriageway nearby and the isolated lights of houses gave the feeling of looking down at the stars, almost a galaxy at your feet. In a gap in the tall hedge one man looked at the view impassively. He leant against his car without seeing the beauty. Nerves played on his mind more than anything. His small, taut body tensed, like his car, for action.

Wearing a grey hoodie against the growing cold he stroked the wing of his car almost lovingly and listened. Eventually a single light wound its way up the hill towards him, vanishing and reappearing as it passed gaps and gateways.

The motorbike purred and popped alongside the car. The rider, hidden behind a tinted visor, cast a look over the other man, then his ride. The Mitsubishi Evo 9 was powerful, but the work the owner had done made the dark purple rally car look even more menacing, hugging the ground like a limpet. Big tyres on big wheels showing massive brakes inside, and everything about it spoke of one purpose: speed. It was a pure-bred racer.

The biker flipped his visor up and nodded to the driver. As he got into his car the other man glanced at his opponent for tonight. A bright red Ducati, tuned, and every bit as fierce as his Evo, but smaller, lighter and more agile.

Flipping his visor down the biker revved his small, fast engine. The car rumbled in return. With a quick hand signal they counted down silently, released their clutches, and left three black lines on the faded tarmac. The bike took an early lead, the car trying to get its weight up to speed. The first corner and the car had caught up, trying to pass. The biker ignored his mirrors, eyes fixed on the next corner, then the next, squeezing every drop of skill from himself and power from his bike. In the car, the air con was off, and the driver sweated as he fought inertia and gravity to chase the red bike down. Neither noticed the headlights slowly catching them from behind.

A tight right, then left, like a chicane on a race circuit, and the car made its move. The biker shut the door on him, forcing the driver to brake hard, falling back. Down the hill, away from the town, the pace quickened. The driver sensed the end soon, the junction marking the finish line drawing near. He let out a deep breath and floored the accelerator. The bike was trying, but on the downhill straight the car was catching. Only three more corners then the line. The bike held the inside on the first left but was at risk on the long right after. Seeing his moment the driver flicked the four-wheel drive racer into the left, kicking out the back end, then switching to the right. He took the bike on the inside, forcing it wide, but not wide enough. The road was too narrow for a car sideways and a bike. With a deep thud that could be felt through the wheel the tail of the Evo hit the side of the bike. Struck on his right leg, the biker felt a giant hand try to push him away, and in desperation grabbed futilely for the carbon boot spoiler of the car, before being thrown hard into the thick hedge. Regaining control the driver slid to a stop and ran back. The bike lay upside down against a small tree, silent and steaming. The rider was gone. Searching frantically the driver found no sign, until he realised he was looking too far ahead. The biker hadn't gone with his bike. A giant old tree, solid and unmoving, had stopped him dead. The body lay in a crumpled heap, like a puppet with its strings cut. The red helmet, matching the bike, was cracked in two like an egg, grey mush exposed. Struggling not to throw up, the driver staggered back to his idling car and raced off, past the finish line, and away.

  The lights behind caught up, stopped by the body of the biker. The driver's window opened a crack, then closed and the car followed the Evo.

  The alarm clock buzzed, the noise a chainsaw to the sleeping form. A hand waved from the depths of a duvet, missed a few times before slapping the snooze button.

Straining and stretching the naked muscular body of Terrence Belkin slid from the comfort of his bed, and sat on the side, rubbing his eyes.

"Why do I get up?" he asked the empty flat. Still rubbing his face he stood, and hobbled over to the toilet, letting out a contented sigh as he emptied the night's urine collection. Leaving the seat up he washed his hands and face and examined himself in the dirty mirror. The man staring back looked tired, and so it should, up all night playing silly buggers. The bad dreams didn't help. Not the ones from before. New ones, fresh and horrid. After picking up his razor, a quick shave, and then dropping it back into the glass by the sink he padded barefoot into the kitchen and hunted for a clean bowl. After a fruitless search, he pulled down a box of cereal and poured the milk straight into it. The lumpy goo smelt worse than it looked, so he dropped the whole thing onto the rubbish pile surrounding the bin. Another take out breakfast. The alarm screamed the passing of ten minutes and Terrence, or 'Tez' as he used to be known, went back to the bed, turned off the alarm, and dressed.

Leaving his tiny studio flat, wondering if he should bother to lock it, Tez half fell down the steps to the line of garage units facing the three-storey block of flats. Most were tatty, some still open. One was clean, smart and very secure. Checking the three padlocks, and the alarm sensor, Tez was satisfied it was safe and walked away. Under the steps was his bike, an unexciting but sufficient Honda CBR 600. A bit tatty and worn, but an ideal daily runner. Zipping his black bike jacket against the morning chill Tex swung his leg over and waddled the bike to the road. The neighbours hated the sound of his bike warming up under their doormats at six in the morning, so he rolled down the road a little, and then started the

Honda by the bus shelter. The other blocks of flats hid the morning rays of warming sun, but the sky was clearing, and it promised to be another warm and sunny day. Glad he had his Kevlar bike jeans Tez let the bike warm until the revs dropped, then pulled on his helmet and rode away.

Behind the only row of shops on Lower Hampton's sleepy high street was a narrow alleyway barely big enough for a small lorry. Down the tight entrance were the premises of Thornton and Hopdyke Motor Services. The unassuming alley hid the size of the garage. With a paint booth, fabrication shop, parts shop on the high street, and all your major mechanical requirements under one roof, it employed twelve staff, including three in the shop. Tez, being multi skilled in all areas of the internal combustion engine, worked all over. The rumour was old man Hopdyke was going to make him a business partner. Tez didn't deny or accept the story, but he had no interest in business. Getting up to his shoulders in a lame engine was his life, and he lived it to the full here.

Cutting the engine as he pulled off the high street Tez rolled the bike around the back of the shops, letting momentum carry him. Gently squeezing the front brake with two fingers, he coasted to a stop by the big roller shutter on the paint booth. Part of the credence to the partner story was Tez having the paint shop keys. Even old Thornton, who rarely visited the garage, had to admit Tez knew how to paint. He could take a crumpled wreck and make it like new. Pulling the key from his jeans pocket Tez unlocked the shutter and slid it up. It rolled near silently, more of his handiwork, and Tez pushed his bike inside, parking it on the mucky spot he did every day. As he turned off the intruder alarm, flicked on the lights

and turned on the kettle, Tez glanced to the paint booth. While the water boiled, he opened the thick insulated door, letting warm, fumed air out. Inside was a smashed Ferrari, old but still valuable, that had been remade into the gleaming classic that now basked under the bright fluorescent strip lights. Peeling the plastic masking off gently Tez laid a soft hand on the repainted flank of the car, not out of reverence, but checking the finish. After a quick break to make a big mug of tea he
7returned, mug in one hand, the other stroking the painted panels. Satisfied, he gave it a final wipe down and wondered where he put the keys.

The sound of an engine pulled him outside. It wasn't a normal car, sounded tuned. Downing the tea Tez headed into the growing dawn, annoyed that his chance to leave the Ferrari in the morning sun to show his boss was being delayed. The dark purple Evo caught his eye at first, then the blue club sticker on the rear quarter lights held him locked. The big number 4 in a solid disc of colour, the letters almost formal after. 4power. The one group Tez wanted to avoid. Keeping himself looking relaxed and unimpressed he leant against the shutter runner, empty mug still in hand as the car tried to park. Why would the 4power crew be after him? Did they know of his hidden secret in the garage? He had been so careful. The driver, in a grey hoodie and a face like death, slowly got out of the car and looked over the smooth roof.

"You Tez?" he asked. Sounded tired, very tired.

"Yeah," Tez tried to sound confident. "Why you asking?"

The man almost smiled, relief lighting his darkened face. "I need a repair job, fast."

Curiosity overcoming caution Tez put his mug on a shelf and walked over.

"Wassup?" he asked when he got close.

"Clipped a post last night. Need a dent and scuff removing." The man gestured to the left rear. Sure enough, there on the angled body was a deep, narrow dent, like the mark left from a pole. But Tez had seen a lot of accident damage. The red mashed into the deep metallic purple paint, the scratches lower down, the smaller dent near the back door. "You can fix it?" the man asked nervously.

"Sure," said Tez. "Can do anything." He looked over the car, checking the brakes' manufacturer, the stance of the car, the cleanliness of the large bore exhaust tip. "Nice wheels. Fast?"

"Yeah." The man relaxed, back on home turf. "Fastest around here. Nothing can touch on the corners. Custom camber kits, coilovers, struts, engine mounts, even the block is re-bored."

"Nice," said Tez again, and looked closer at the damaged rear corner. "Leave me a number and I'll price it up when the boss gets here. He goes ape if I do it alone. Says I'm stealing his custom." Tez laughed. The man didn't.

"Anyway, won't be much."

"Can't you do it now?" the man asked, nervous again.

"I can, but I'll get the boot. You're lucky, car I was doing is finished. Can get it in first thing; be ready by early afternoon, provided you have the cash."

The man nodded, scribbled his number, no name, and left like a soldier in a battle zone. Tez watched him and felt the need for another cup of tea. Refilled mug in hand he wandered to the car, still feeling uncertain. Finally, he wheeled his bike over, putting it near the back of the race car. Like a jigsaw puzzle the marks matched near perfect. Unless the post was motorbike shaped, he had hit a biker, and at speed. Putting the bike back Tez found the Ferrari keys and drove the classic into the sunniest part of the yard, right where Hopdyke would see it when he came in, putting the Evo to the back of his mind. He had to clean the booth before he could do anything anyway.

The old man was, as usual, muted in his approval. A quiet nod and mumbled praise were the best you could get. Tez was happy he had done a good job, the opinions of others secondary. He argued over the Evo until Hopdyke pulled rank and insisted a scuffed Mercedes had first view. It was a simple car park scrape, probably against another car. Tez noted how close the seat was to the steering wheel, the electric adjust pedals raised. Meant a shorter driver in a very big car. Tez was sanding the panel ready to filler and prime when a rumble in the yard made him lift his head from the car. A black Range Rover had parked next to the Evo. Something niggled at him, the car didn't seem right.

The driver of the big luxury car didn't seem too interested in anything. He sat behind the wheel, V8 engine burbling. Tez dropped the sandpaper back into the water bucket and wiped his hands. The driver still didn't move. Everyone seemed busy; Hopdyke hated leaving customers unattended more than a minute. 'Leave them alone too long and they decide to drop the price,' he used to say almost as if from some old bible scripture. With a moan of irritation Tez threw the drying rag on a shelf as he walked into the mid-morning sun.

The car still idled, a small, thin cloud of steam vapour curling from the stainless-steel exhaust. As he got closer, Tez clicked. The car was old, maybe twenty years; there had certainly been a couple of newer models since this was made. There were dents, scuffs and marks all over its large, black panels. The wheels were standard 20-inch fitments, but there the differences stood out. The tyres were near slick racing tread, fitting almost inside the arches like the air suspension had collapsed. Through the spokes were massive 8 pot callipers, painted black as well, on racing discs hiding the chrome suspension. The exhaust, rich and fruity some would say, spoke of tuned power, a slight whine said supercharger. This was no mud plugger, or rich man's poser. This was a car made for speed, power and strength. There wasn't a tow bar fitted, but recovery shackles hung under the tatty bumpers. The more he looked, the more Tez was lost as to why the owner had done this to an old four by four.

The window glass was mildly tinted, hiding detail, but still showing the driver sat as if asleep. Tez stood where he would be seen, then, when he saw the man still not move he gently tapped the glass. The man raised one finger to say 'wait'. Still looking for clues Tez looked over the car again. The drivers' door opened, and the man finally got out. Tez felt even more confused at his appearance. Unlike the outside of his car the man was neat, tidy and fairly smart. His trainers were clean, the dark jeans stain free, polo shirt without creases and the blonde-haired face neatly shaven. Inside the car looked spotless, showroom fresh. The driver shut the door before Tez could get a good look, but he saw something non factory on the dash, and what looked like an extra aerial in the door frame.

"Terrence Belkin?" he asked.

"Yeah, why?" Tez went straight into defence mode. This was official speak.

"Inspector Henderson, crime." The inspector held out a police badge and ID in a beige holder. "Just a few questions, nothing you've done wrong." he smiled. That made it worse.

"About what?" Tez asked, leaning back against the Evo, trying to look calm.

"That car, actually," Henderson said. Tez moved aside as the inspector walked around the car as if he was considering buying it. Tez followed like a salesman.

"Not mine." Tez felt guilt, and a need to explain before this copper came to the wrong conclusion.

Henderson shot him a curious look. Under his cold grey eyes they seemed to probe into his mind, giving Tez a headache.

"Of course not," the blonde policeman smiled his unsettling smile. "We know who, and we know where he lives. I'm more bothered about why it's here, not halfway over town."

Tez shrugged. As police questions went, this was seriously strange. The fashionable copper was almost rubbing his nose on the bonnet of the car, looking into the purple paint as if trying to see the engine through it. Maybe he could. Tez suddenly felt naked and exposed, like his very soul was on trial and open for the world to see. He resisted the urge to put his hands over his crotch. Instead he took a half breath and leant on the warm wing of the Range Rover.

"So if you know where he is, Inspector, why are you here?"

Henderson stood so quickly Tez jumped. "I know where he is, Belkin, but I want to know why his car isn't with him. When did it come in?"

"This morning, first thing. I came in early to take a car out of the booth and he came in shortly after."

Henderson cocked his head slightly. "Just after you?"

"Yeah. About ten minutes or so. I'd just finished opening up. Check the cameras if you want."

The inspector held his clean hands out as if warding off a dangerous dog. "No need. I believe you. Why did he bring it?"

"Scuff on the back end," Tez pointed unnecessarily to the scrape. Henderson seemed to have just noticed the damage despite having walked past it, on his side of the car.

"Nasty one, eh?" he touched the dent, tracing the deeper scratches with one finger. After doing nearly everything but lick the car Henderson stood and faced Tez. The taller, tanned copper looked down at Tez, more than just physically. After another radar sweep with those grey eyes neither man flinched, although Tez shivered openly under the gaze. Henderson grunted, doubt briefly clouding his face. Without a word he pushed past Tez, got back into his car, and drove away. The yard felt ten degrees colder, even after the engine note had passed through the alley, paused on the high street, then rumbled off, shouting power and purpose to the ancient streets. Tez leant against the Evo to steady himself. From his office Hopdyke banged on the window, waving Tez back to work. With a shrug he went back inside, pausing to glance over his shoulder at the purple street racer with the dent in the back.

2

Down the high street, away from the shops, was a left turn out of town. Past the slightly run down council accommodation and around the half built new housing estate, but before you left town was the large, wood and brick public house, the Black Bull. As typical as an

English pub could be, they had beer on tap, cider and lager in bottles, vodka and spirits on the wall behind the bar, a pool table, jukebox and a fireplace. It stank of stale beer, smoke and sweat. The bar was the usual mix of light and dark wood, with a bronzed rail running around the edge, high bar stools standing like sentinels. The main taps, condensation running down their chromed necks, held name tags like medals. The dented and scuffed dark wood of the bar's surface was covered in rubber beer mats and peanut bowls. From behind the empty bar two voices argued, one older and male, one younger and female.

"Damn it, girl, I changed your nappies when you were born, but I don't need to see it now!"

"See what?"

"Every bloody thing! Can't you wear a skirt that covers your lady parts, or at least knickers? Damn it, your mother would turn in her grave."

"Don't drag mum into this. You know she wore most of this herself."

"True, but she wasn't flashing her parts to her own dad".

"Awe, c'mon Daddy."

"Don't give me the little girl act, now get your slutty ass up them steps. Sort the bottles in the fridges and fill the snacks up. And get some bloody clothes on. We ain't a brothel."

A blonde head appeared jerkily over the bar as the girl walked up the cellar steps. Short, but well-proportioned she knew how to use her body, making more in tips than wages, not that her dad paid much anyway.

"Christine!" yelled her father from the depths.

She stamped on the floor with a high heel, more from frustration than to make a noise. "What?"

"Don't forget to unlock the doors too. Must be opening time soon."

"Yes, Dad." She stomped as loudly as possible to the end of the bar, lifted the end up and crossed the silent pub to the main door. Flicking the bolts and locks she tugged the old wooden doors open, letting the warm morning air in. Her dad emerged from the cellar, balancing four packs of beer cans on his gut, trying not to topple backwards. Christie giggled, earning another furious look.

"Well help me then, damn it. Don't giggle like a schoolgirl. Did sod all in school but chase boys anyway."

"Yes, Dad."

"Yes, Dad," he mimicked, and dropped the cans on the bar before Christie reached him. "Man, we need some extra help." He wiped sweat from his forehead with his shirtsleeve, already wet from numerous wipes.

"Or lose weight, tubby," Christie said, playfully. She swept past him as he made a weak attempt to play slap her arm. Both stopped when the rumble of a car engine slowed outside, floating through the open door. They looked at each other, silently praying it would move on. It didn't. The sound of tyres on gravel, then silence. A door opened, closed. Christie looked to her father, who nodded to the bar.

Hide.

The doorway, in the shade of the sun, darkened as a figure walked in. The muscular, tattooed man looked almost like a one-man riot.

"Barkeep," he spoke softly, near a whisper.

"Mr. Hopwood."

The man smiled, sat on one of the bar stools, leaning on the bar like a friendly local. The sweat on the barkeepers' head started to run again.

"Barkeep, I fancy a cold drink."

"Certainly, sir." A pint was hurriedly poured into a clean glass and placed on the unmarked rubber mat. The man watched as the liquid went from foamy cream to dark brown.

"Where's that pretty daughter of yours?" he asked, still staring at the drink.

"Busy," the response too quick. The man looked up from the drink.

"Busy? Too busy for your favourite customer?" said Hopwood almost accusingly. "You know, Alvin, I hope you remember all I have done for you here."

"Of course, Mr. Hopwood, and I am very grateful."

"I think you really are," said Hopwood. He took a long draw on the pint, letting it slide down. When he put the glass back it was half full. He wiped the foam moustache with a bar napkin. "I just popped by to see if tonight's game was still on?"

"Of course, Mr Hopwood. Highlight of my week is poker night." There was little enthusiasm in his voice. Hopwood noticed.

"You will be joining us?"

"Of course." Alvin forced a smile. "Think my luck is changing."

"Good. How much for the drink?"

Alvin, being practised this routine, waved a hand dismissively. "On the house, to our best customer."

"Cheers, Barkeep," Hopwood said, slapping Alvin's arm. He drained the glass and left.

Christie emerged from behind the bar. "Why do you play against him? He cheats and you know it."

"Yeah," sighed her father. "But I owe him a lot, and he gets funny if I refuse. I need to win some games to pay him back."

"How deep are we, Dad?"

"Deep enough to worry," Alvin looked at his feet, turned and went back down to the cellar. Christie looked at the empty glass with almost loathing, feeling the urge to throw it through the open door, but put it in the dishwasher anyway.

Outside the engine started and drove away.

Tez sat at the table nearest the window. He liked watching the traffic, the people, the world. Also being near the window, and the door, meant he was near the exit should anyone he didn't want to meet turned up. He munched his large bacon and sausage sandwich, or batch as they locally called them, and watched the world coast by. Lower Hampton wasn't big, and definitely not known for good food establishments. You could head to the retail park, get your fast food or mass made pizzas, but for a classic greasy spoon your best bet was a few miles down the dual carriageway. Tez had tried the café next to the shop out of idleness, and found the food was better than he was led to believe. His craving for fried food, bacon and egg especially, was satisfied. Now with a wholemeal roll (healthy don't you know?) holding five large rashers of crispy bacon, and four sausages, halved, he felt a happy man.

The owner of the Evo, Henderson's target, hadn't come back yet. The car was sat in the booth, baking. The Ferrari was long gone to an almost tearful owner, and the black Range Rover hadn't been seen. As he ate Tez watched the traffic drive past. A few cars did catch his eye, a Ford Focus ST, slammed to the floor bellowing from an oversized exhaust, a Mazda RX7 tastefully done, with wide body arches, ready to drift. Also a few bikes, mostly sports bikes, GSXR's, Ninjas and Blades, blasted by. One Ducati vibrated the windows with its deep twin tone exhaust. Tez knew there was no love lost between bikers and car drivers. Personally he sat on the fence. Bikes were fast, some stupidly fast, but vulnerable. Cars were safer, but heavier. The winner of a race would be more down to the operator, than the machine.

The thought of racing made him cease chewing his food, look down instinctively. It was racing that had brought him here, not to race, but to escape the world of carbon brakes, superchargers, nitrous oxide and neon lights. As a young kid he always loved cars, like you do. Nobody ever went without at least a dozen toy cars when he was a boy, mostly unimpressive metal die cast with the name and model on the poor imitation chassis. Tez had a fleet. His dad liked fast bikes, his mum not so much. His dad had taken a young Tez to bike races; Moto GP, British super bikes, Isle of Man TT. Anything with two wheels was his utopia. There was an old BMW katana in the garage. Together they rebuilt it and rode the country roads as soon as Tez could reach the foot pegs. His mum was quiet, but he could tell she didn't like it.

In school he dreamed of racing, being one of the guys leaning his bike almost onto its side into the deep corners, scraping knee and elbow sliders on the super grip tarmac. He started to take more interest in school, especially maths, science and engineering. By the age of twelve it seemed he had chosen his career. Tez started junior motorbike racing. He won a lot, mostly down to the meticulous care he took setting his tiny 250cc bike to each track, walking the circuit to learn it while the other kids slept. The progress to the bigger 500cc class seemed assured, maybe even a top spot. Tragedy struck in one race near the end of the season. Tez was just fourteen, being watched by a scout he knew could help his dream to become a reality. Pushing hard Tez took pole, and in the race dominated, lapping the slower riders. One didn't see him coming, cut the apex, low siding his bike and pitching Tez screaming into the air. He landed in the gravel, one leg bent backwards, unconscious. He woke in hospital with a massive headache, and his right side in plaster. The doctors said he would heal, a fractured pelvis at his age shouldn't slow him much, but to this day he walked with a slight limp, and his career ended in the gravel trap. He still shook hands with the other kid, forgiving him.

A year out of school did nothing to curb his spirit. Once walking again he decided bikes were fun, but not for him. He turned to four wheels and once he left school he went first to college to get some practical qualifications, then university, all the way up in Edinburgh, studying motor racing for his degree. Out of the classroom his mind seemed to explode, craving any scrap of info it could find. He watched every race from touring cars to Formula One, looking at set-ups, track layouts, strategies. In the class he became a handful, asking a lot of questions. With the expansion of the internet Tez found a fountain of information. This led to his discovery.

By the end of the 20th century carbon, especially carbon fibre, had become the big thing in car manufacture. Ferrari pioneered the F40, a mostly carbon fibre car, and the turn of the millennium made carbon fibre a boom market. Street racers, bikers, astronauts, scientists, explorers, all wanted this light weight material for their equipment. Tez looked into the possibility of using it to lessen the biggest weight in a car, the engine and gearbox. With some tweaking, and help from a friend in the science lab, Tez managed to come up with the formula for the perfect engine, more powerful, more economical, and weighing in at a tenth of it's equivalent performer. He rushed the designs through, making a working miniature, and peddled it around the car manufacturers nearby. The response was unanimous, and shocking. Not interested.

   Dejected, Tez decided to prove them all wrong. He went back to the science lab and with a little bribery to smooth the way made a full sized working engine and gearbox suitable for a mid sized family saloon car. With some fabrication he fitted it to a cheap car he found, almost scaring himself silly when he realised what he had made.
With some fettling to the brakes and suspension Tez found a cheap family run-around that could sit behind race cars and still do nearly a hundred miles to the gallon. A few track days showing his car blast past Lamborghini's and Porsches sealed it for him. Tez put his peddling shoes back on and went back to the manufacturers. They were more interested, but still unimpressed. Too experimental they kept repeating.

   Twice a failure Tez gave in. He considered scrapping the car and going back to his studies. A small detour to a street race meet changed it all. One short race and he had finally found his place. Setting the car perfectly he could beat anything, and did. Winning a lot of money he slipped easily into the murky underworld of street racing; the drink, girls, thrills and drugs. Ditching university Tez lived off his winnings. His parents were at first shocked, then upset, finally angry. He had brought disgrace on the family name, and his car was an embarrassment. Tez tried to explain the genius of his creation, but on deaf ears. Even when his father offered to help try and sell it to the big car makers again Tez refused. He'd had enough of the corporate world. He loved racing. He wanted to go professional and said so, but both his mum, upset, and his dad, frustrated, ordered him back to university. The row woke the neighbours, the scream of Tez's exhaust woke the street. He never went home again, his parents distanced themselves from him.

His sister, so hugely offended by her bigger brother, did the cruellest thing she could, blocked him on Facebook.

Alone with his gang Tez won race after race, rising to semi pro on the underground circuit. He was being noticed, but by the good and bad. Fights were common, drink flowed and the girls were willing. He was happy, but that was shattered by three large police investigators, and a man from the income tax office. His cash was seized, a small stash of drugs meant a night in the cells, and a permanent record. In that tiny 5x6 white painted room Tez saw his future, and cried. Once out he swore never to return. He received a caution for the drugs, a slap on the wrist form the tax man, and a lift home from the chief. his flat, cleaned out by revenue, Tez packed his few remaining things, left the key on the kitchen counter, and walked out, taking his small stash of money, escape money. He texted his group, those out on bail, then threw away his phone. Heading off he abandoned his previous life and ran.

Now, months later, he had drifted into lower Hampton, found a job at the garage, made a home and settled. The bike was a cheap buy, sold locally by some kid who had just got a full sized sports bike. The prototype car hid like a sleeping monster in the dark of the garage, tank full of Tez's home brew of 98 Ron petrol, paraffin, some special sauce and preservers. Should he need to leave fast again, he was ready.

3

The town nestled in the centre of a crescent of hills, blocking the west wind, and catching the sun for most of the day. Some intelligent council official had checked the terrain and found the best place for a scenic picnic spot. There were now tables with benches, a toilet block, and bins. In the car park overlooking the town, a motorbike sat, rider laid out in the afternoon sun, jacket rolled up under his head.

He was a small, almost weedy man, with long dark hair puddling over his bright red leather jacket like a waterfall. Scars on his right arm showed where surgeons had to insert metal into broken bones. His pale and weak appearance, made worse by the skin tight bike leather he wore, hid the truth; he was the boss, the head man. On his legs, black on the bright red, was the Japanese logo, and lettering, of the largest biker gang around, the Yoki Riders. Mark Hopwood ran it, and ran it well. Social events, charity bike washes and community work, most agreed that the bikes were loud and dangerous, but the people who rode them were nice.

Mark was well liked, unlike his younger brother.

The rumble of the car mingled with the crunch of gravel. Mark didn't move. Colin stood over his older brother, almost with disgust. A year stood between them, but the differences were massive. Colin dwarfed Mark. He was tattooed, muscular and clean shaven. He ran the 4power crew, and ran them hard. Whereas Mark got along with jokes, laughs and expedience, Colin ruled with fear and intimidation. That had led to their argument, and finally, the war.

Ten years ago, when Colin turned 21 they both went out for a race. Colin preferred cars, mostly as Mark was a biker. They raced what they had, an old jelly mould CBR and a Ford Escort RS turbo. The race was a draw. Colin argued he had won, but their friends had said no, even a photo of them crossing the line did nothing to change Colin's mind. He swore revenge, and every year they raced. Both wanted the town, the control of the roads. Racing between groups was forbidden, even relaxed Mark insisted on that. Once a year, in the summer, they met at the old airfield south of town, and the grudge matches were played out. Biker cut you up? Car blocked your bike in? Settle it then. After ten years they hadn't decided the biggest grudge. Story was Colin was getting desperate. Mark knew his brother, and it scared him inside.

"See you still can't stay off your back," Colin grunted, looking over his brothers bike.

"Nope," said Mark, his eyes still closed.

"You heard?"

Mark nodded. He knew Colin would be annoyed at his lack of interest, and forced down a grin.

"So?" Colin kicked some gravel that rattled off Mark's helmet.

"So nothing." Mark sat upright, looking over the town. "They did it, not us. Let it go."

"I can't." Colin was angry. He walked in front of Mark, almost leaning into his older brother's pale face. "You know the rules. No racing out of the field."

Mark shrugged. "They did a little test ride."

"Test ride!?" Colin threw his hands into the air, turning away. Dropping his shoulders he tried a different approach. "One of yours died. Don't you care?"

"Of course I do. It was stupid of Mickey to have done it, and your guy. But nothing we can do will bring him back. He's another of the honoured dead."

Colin looked ready to strike. His face was dark, beads of

sweat on his brow. Mark never got angry, and that wound him up the most.

"Col, listen, it happened. I told mine not to retaliate. We ain't gonna have another riot like last time, so chill it."

Colin walked off, muttering 'chill it' under his breath. He yanked his door open and turned back. "If we have another war, brother, it will be on your hands, not mine." He slammed the door before Mark could respond and drove away, covering Mark in a cloud of dust.

Shaking his head sadly Mark waited for the engine noise to die out completely. Then he stood, shook the dust from his jacket, pulled his hair back into it's usual ponytail, tucked it under his jacket, and sat on the bike. With a lingering look over the town he slid his helmet on, walked the bike backwards and fired it up.

"That went well," he said inside his helmet, kicked the bike into gear and rode slowly away.

The rest of the week passed as many others had before. The guy turned up for his Evo, paid more than he should have, and left. Tez had no end of strange cars with strange marks to fix, clean, tune and repair, but none that looked like accident damage. Shutting at four on Saturday afternoon Tez reflected, as he usually did, on the week before. Aside from that creepy Monday nothing was different, but it felt strange. Almost like a premonition he felt something stirring, the way animals know an earthquake is coming, or plants know when the rain is due. Something ate at him inside, but he ignored it, thinking it only nerves. He was so very wrong.

Near the northern borders of the town, but far enough from the shopping centre to the west not to be congested come closing time, another garage was being closed, but not all of it. The unassuming façade of Crippin's

Motorcycle Repair and Service premises looked like any other bike repair garage, but behind was a smooth, grippy tarmac yard with a small clubhouse and bar, the evening haunt of the Yoki Riders. Mark Hopwood leant on his bike, jacket open to the afternoon breeze, and listened to the rich sound of revving engines, friendly banter and good times. A cold beer in his right hand, left on the handlebar, he was a happy man. The girls were still showing it all off, competing with the chrome and steel 'ladies' the men rode. Some girls rode too, tattoos and piercings of a biker chick. Most rode bitch though, happy it seemed to let their bodies compete. Sometimes they did bikini contests here, or bikini washes for charity. The proposed and failed Miss Lower Hampton competition would have been held in the small back yard, but the council ruled it out. Shame, as there were plenty of willing competitors, and spectators. By the end of the night at least one guy would have a bleeding nose, one girl be topless, and a few guys get lucky. For now though it was beer and banter time.

Mel Telford was nearly topless already, her usual cut off shirts a little shorter than usual. No guys were trying for those half eclipsed breasts, most thought her a rug muncher. Mark spied Claire Hook walking towards him, hips wiggling in hot pants. That meant Petey must be nearby. They never went far apart.

"Yo, boss." The voice of Petey Kenner dragged Mark's eyes from the appealing form of Claire.

"Wassup, Petey?"

"Just wondering, you know, about Mickey?"

Mark dropped the permanent smile on his face, clouded and dark in the sun.

"He did wrong. A shame, but can't change that."

Petey turned to watch the gang, some already getting a

bit rough. Neither looked at each other. Claire hugged Petey's arm like a lifeline.

"Thing is, boss, what about the grudge match? You know your bro ain't gonna back down, and he sure as hell ain't gonna let this drop."

Mark shook his head. "I spoke to Colin. I said to drop it. He ain't happy, but he'll keep schtum. I'm more worried about filling his slot. We need a good circuit man. Mickey was the best we had."

"Nobody worth shit compared to Mickey," Petey admitted.

"You volunteering?"

"No way, Boss." Claire held his arm tighter, making Petey almost shout the words.

Mark picked up his discarded smile and faced his number two.

"Well, we have to go on. Sod it. Let's get smashed."

Petey paused for a moment, looking into the face of the man he had known from school. Finally he nodded, smiled himself, and the three went to the bar. It was impossible with that face to stay sad for long. It got you in the end.

South of the bikers the Black Bull was also packed, not with locals, they stayed away. Cars filled the gravel car park, so low they nearly touched the light stone chips. Bass thumped with enough strength the earth moved. Lights danced with the beat, and girls danced with the lights. Heels so high they looked like stilts, skirts so short they hid little, and not much on above. These were also competing with their men's chosen transport, a small world of neon, sub woofers, and beer, of course. The guys, mostly all drivers were male, wandered about in small groups, some with a girl or two keeping their arms warm. They looked over the latest modifications, trends and styles. The girls just danced and flirted, craving attention.

Near the open door to the pub, but away from the picnic benches down the side, three cars were parked in the best space. One was the dark grey Nissan Skyline of Colin Hopwood. Wheels spread wide, aerodynamic body kit, large boot spoiler and massive brakes. It was made to beat anything, in a straight, or cornered race. For the past three years it had faced the bikes his brother fielded, and drawn every race. Now Mark had the new bike, a supercharged bike, Colin knew his wouldn't win. This put him in a foul mood. Martin, the unofficial second, tried to talk him out, but even with a stream of beer Colin held his dark, withdrawn mood. One foolish girl tried to talk, and nearly somersaulted off her heels when he shoved her away. Since then everyone left him alone.

"Bleeding Ritchie," he said eventually.

"That twat?" asked Martin, then wished he hadn't.

Colin turned so violently Martin thought he would lash out.

"Yes, that twat. Who the fuck else?"

"Wh-what about him?" Martin tried to back off, but he was next to his Audi and trapped.

"Wh-what about him? Dip shit nearly started another war. You want that? He bloody well did. And now he's gonna pay. If he ever shows."

Martin knew Ritchie would be a million miles away if he had any brains, but he wasn't known for that. Skill with a car, that Evo able to run like it was on rails, and a strong drinkers gut, yes. But brains? No luck there.

As if on cue the Evo purred slowly into the car park, past the now silent and still people, and stopped in front of the Skyline. After a moment's thought Ritchie got out, and with head held down, stood before Colin, who looked rather pleased.

"Look who it is, everyone!" Colin called loudly. Those showing off their sound systems turned them down. They had seen this mood before, and knew it best to play along. They had no official membership, but this was as close to being thrown out as you could be.

Ritchie kept his head down, silent.

"Wassup, Ritchie? Kitty cat got your tongue?" Colin asked, not looking at the man's head

Still looking down Ritchie mumbled an apology. Colin sprang forwards like a coiled snake, squaring off to the man, shoulders raised, muscles ready.

"You what?"

"I said, I'm sorry for causing aggro on the hill. Didn't mean to do wrong, both for you, and the club," Ritchie was nearly in tears, but he looked up into the face of his leader, then dropped it immediately. Colin seemed to grow, like an eagle spreading it's wings over a small mouse.

"You are sorry?"

Ritchie just nodded, staring at the shoes of Colin.

"Well, then. That's ok. He said sorry, guys! All forgiven."

The crowd were uneasy. This never happened, even when Colin was drunk. There must be some trick. Ritchie, who had seen it all before, kept his head down.

Colin started to walk away, then turned and struck. His fist flew in a blur, catching Ritchie perfectly in the jaw, lifting him off his feet and onto the bonnet of his car. He coughed and spat two teeth. Trying to roll away he was stopped by a hammer blow to his belly, creasing him in two. In his small world of pain he heard glass breaking. Colin tore at the car with venom. Every window with the club sticker on was smashed, every panel scraped clear of any connection. When he was done his breath came in deep and hard. The car looked like it had been in a demolition derby.

"Ritchie?" Colin asked, bending low over the still foetus-like prone body. "Ritchie?" he almost sang the words.

"Yeah, Colin?" he managed, spitting blood.

"Go fuck yourself, and never come in this town again." Colin gave him a last kick in the kidneys, that made everyone cringe, then turned away. Christie handed him a beer as he passed, ignoring the hand that grabbed a tit. At least he wouldn't break any more windows. Ritchie struggled to his feet, and without a word got into his wrecked car and left.

4

Inspector Henderson waved his key fob at the door lock, and pushed the door open. The front of the tiny police station was an old red brick house like most of the buildings on the main street. The reception, offices and toilets were near the front, the station was deceptively deep from the front to the back. In the rear was a small yard for the two official liveried Vauxhall Vectras, one Land Rover Discovery, and an unmarked Skoda Octavia VRS. The cells, holding area, interview rooms and analysis room were almost in a separate area. It all smelt of dust, stale clothes and age. Henderson hated the smell, like in his most hated old school. He felt the same about the station to be honest, too small for him to make his mark in the force.

At 48 the inspector wasn't old, but by now should have

done what he was going to do to get promoted. He had been working in Birmingham, implementing the new rules set out a few years ago, stopping street racing and bad boy racers by making it illegal for them to meet anywhere. It worked. Too well. Street racing was dead in the Black Country and Henderson had no crime to fight. When he heard of a gang war in a town east of him he jumped at the chance by transferring without looking. Big mistake. The gang war turned out to be two stupid brothers who had a falling out years ago, and now fought over the town. With no law stopping them meeting he could only drive past and do nothing, except be laughed at.

Henderson shoved a door harder than he needed to, ignoring the processing sergeant, who always made a joke at his expense, and went into his office. The desk was clean and clear, testament to his thorough and meticulous organisation. He often reflected inwardly he had an OCD about being tidy, even making his desk line up neatly with the wall of the office, his computer screen aligned with the window overlooking the side street that looped the station. His Range Rover lay sleeping alongside, a leopard awaiting a foolish gazelle. Henderson faced away from the door to the station where fools in uniform chased small crooks committing small crimes in a small town. He had no pictures on his desk, or his walls. The car outside was all he wanted. Divorced, his ex couldn't handle his dedication to his job.

Childless by the grace of God. He had a tidy semi detached house in the new build area in the north of the town, and together with his car and his job he had what he needed.

Some at the station who tried to befriend him were puzzled by his car. His home, office, even his appearance was clean, tidy and carefully laid out. His car was the opposite. Originally gloss black when it left the Solihull assembly line the wheels had been replaced, with a lot of other parts, by the tuning specialist Overfinch. The 4.6 V8 was swapped for Chevrolet's 7.2 litre supercharged monster. Massive brakes, up rated air bag suspension and a gearbox that would run off an ocean liners engine, kept the big beast on the tarmac. Henderson kept the inside spotless, because it was his own personal space. But outside it looked old and scruffy in order to blend in, and to remain largely unnoticed. Many boy racers had tried and failed to escape the big rectangular grille of Henderson's four by four, on and off road. They never succeeded. The marks were battle scars and he was proud of them.

Leaning back in the non issue Recaro office chair Henderson looked at his car. The look was of love, and nothing else. With a sigh he pulled a folder from a desk drawer, flipping idly through the pages. A knock at the door was openly ignored.

"Hey, Inspector," Constable Bicks poked her pretty head around the door, not opening it in case something attacked her. Henderson just grunted, still gazing over the file. Bicks came in, shutting the door quietly behind her. Sitting opposite him, in front of the window, she waited patiently. Young, only 28, and with rich blonde hair spilling over her shoulder in a ponytail Constable Helen Bicks was very popular, some of their guests in the cells asking for her to be the one to frisk search them. Having joined the Lower Hampton force shortly after Henderson she tried to build a relationship, seeing something in the tall, toned, pale haired man. Others laughed, but wished her well, hoping they could catch her on the rebound. After five years they still hadn't been for even a drink of coffee, and the others gave up waiting. But Helen never did.

"Hey, Inspector? Marv?" she tried again. Still he looked over the file. She knew he had every word memorised. "I was thinking," she said, ignoring him, "that my five year service anniversary is coming up, yours too, so I wanna celebrate. The pub down the road is a decent place. Why not go for one? Celebrate our success?"

Henderson froze, only his eyes moved, straight to hers. She nearly flinched under that look. The grey pupils like icicles aimed at her soft heart.

"Success? What success?" he spat.

Helen nearly spoke, but held it. Calm yourself, she thought.

"Well, Marv," she began.

"I hate 'Marv', Constable Bicks."

Helen coughed. This was going very wrong. Those eyes still pierced her very soul, chilling the room. Her arms covered in goose bumps.

"I, err, I just thought, you know." Mumbling she tried to look away, but couldn't.

"No, I don't. Please enlighten me." Henderson laid the folder neatly in line with the edge of the desk, and folded his arms. Helen felt heat melt the room, heat from inside her.

Her cheeks flushed, temper rising.

"Damn it, Marv, why are you so bleeding cold? You neutered or something?" She stared at the floor, ashamed of her outburst. She sensed him move, not to her, but past to the window.

"Is that all, Constable Bicks?" he asked, looking out the window. Helen stood and left, over her shoulder she saw him staring at his car. That bloody car! Maybe he was one of those freaks who had sex with their car, dreaming they were real, alive. Well, he can marry the bleeding thing for all she cared. Her heart pounding, ache of shame in her gut, she turned away, slamming the door.

   Henderson hardly noticed. He had been in this boring shitty little town for too long, his life, and future drifting by.
He could just slow down, ease back, let the lazy countryside soften him. Allow the locals into his life. But he wanted out. He'd considered requesting a reposting, but the gangs still ran, and that wouldn't fly with him.
   Sitting back down he flipped the file until the picture of the purple Evo came up. Lab tests proved it was the same shade as the one mashed into the bike the Thelwood kid had been riding when he creamed into an oak tree. A thought puzzled his face briefly. Going to the filing cabinet he pulled the folder listing the gang members and their roles or skills in the groups. It had taken time, but Henderson was good and he knew who did what, when and why. Chasing the list with a finger he found the name. Thelwood, Michael. Circuit man. Best at out and out races head to head. Henderson checked the date on his wrist watch. The grudge matches would be in a month or so. Without their best guy the Yoki riders could lose, and that would make things very interesting. The grey eyes lightened slightly, the corners of the mouth creasing into a ghost of a smile. Very interesting indeed.

   That night two lights blasted through the country lanes. A solo racer was putting his car through it's paces, thrashing it hard. Nobody used those roads at night, the tourists, more common as the days warmed, long in their hotel beds, the lovers in theirs, or someone's anyway. The car, silver and black, rocked through the narrow roads, soaking up the rough surface, bumps and undulations.

Spitting loose dirt and gravel on the corners when the car slid into a drift, making the clouds kicked up behind glow red, it shot past the accident point of a week before, police tape still hanging like tinsel on the tree. The road signs at the junction shook slightly as the car fired through and into the night. In a layby a car sat, dark and still. It saw the racer pass, but ignored it. The driver had seen all they wanted to.

  Christie hated Sunday mornings. The pub was always a mess, the gents floor slick with piss, the bar sticky. It took all morning to make it presentable enough to open the doors. Her dad stayed up after closing time, turning the taps off in the cellar, locking all the windows, and putting the till cash into the safe, sending her to bed. Passing his room she saw through the open door her dad asleep, snoring loudly.
Mincing on her toes she crept past so he could sleep. Colin Hopwood was always in a foul mood when he had a fight, and last night was no exception. In a foul mood Colin drank a lot. The only blessing was that he ignored her, downing too many pints without paying, then shooting off in his annoying car.
  In the bar itself Christie avoided the sticky puddles of spilt beer, broken glass and some stuff she didn't want to know what it was. Getting a can of pop from a fridge she drank it down fast, dropping the can into the empty recycling tub. Carrying the grey tub she gathered the bottles and cans lying around, putting the now full tub out back next to the bins. After collecting all the broken glass, two bras and a pair of boxer shorts stuck up on a ceiling light, she mopped the floor, opening the front door to air the room. She nearly screamed when she saw Colin standing there. He looked like crap, like he hadn't

slept. Fear made her tremble, had he come for her?

"Ah, little miss Bitch. Got a job for you, love." He grabbed her arm and pulled her into the pub.

Tez slept very late that Sunday. It was afternoon before his stomach and bladder decided to call it a draw and both woke him. A short internal discussion determined the bladder had priority, and after a toilet break Tez raided the fridge, settling for cheese on toast. Deciding his flat was getting too bad he pulled his dressing gown on, flipped the radio to a local dance station he liked, and armed with a black bin bag he tidied. By five the flat was clean, dusted, shiny. Dishes washed and put away, out of date food in the cupboards put in the food bin. Windows let the clean breeze in, and the sound of a car driving slowly past. Tez looked out of curiosity. A dark grey Skyline cruised slowly past, almost stopping by his flat. Tez watched, gripping the curtain tight. The car nearly stopped, then shot off towards town. Unsettled, Tez looked on his mobile phone for a new lock-up to keep his car. Something smelt funny, and it wasn't his flat.

Henderson was up early. His car was his life, it was his badge of authority. He took great pride and pleasure in it's maintenance. Oil was changed every three months, fuel and air filter every year. The garage attached to his house had been extended back into the long garden, making space for a workbench and rolling tool chest. Parts, old panels, and curios from his past hung on the wall or were neatly arranged on shelves. A large, plain white office clock sat in the centre, accurately depicting the time. Wearing an old t-shirt with oil stains and a few rips, Henderson pulled the injectors, the filter, the dipstick, checking them all. It wasn't due a service yet, but he had the feeling something was coming, like animals know the rains are due. There was going to be a storm, and he would be ready.

5

Monday came as Mondays always do, sudden and uninvited, like an unwelcome relative. Tez woke late, dragging himself out of bed. Dashing across town he got to work just in time, surprising the others who were used to him opening up before they got there. Once the day had started in earnest the usual mix of banter and horseplay ensued. Tools were hidden, parts put in hard to reach places, essential things put high for the shorter guys. Tez ignored them, and was ignored. It wasn't that he was distant and disliked company. Far from it. Back home Tez was the one everyone sought out for help or advice, or to make them laugh. Tez loved being the centre of attention, and in the past had more than his share, that was the problem. Once the law was involved and he ran, he learnt the more you left behind, the harder it was to stay away. Sometimes he drove back home, rolling slowly down the familiar streets, but never to the old haunts, or old friends. If he had to run again, he would do it with little baggage.

If asked his co-workers would say Tez was clever, but strange. Half were jealous of his skill, his intuition. Others were puzzled why a good looking guy lived in a poky little flat by himself. Half the women in town would love to warm his bed, even the married ones. Something was wrong with that one, they said. Old man Hopdyke figured his young genius was more than a little disturbed, some bad history. He was closest, but Tez wouldn't talk and Hopdyke grew bored easily. So Tez was left out of work parties, social events, even the Christmas secret Santa. They left him to work, and he was fine with that. Not happy, but fine.

The sun flew overhead in a flat arc, shining on one wall of the yard, then changing it's mind half way through the day and lighting the other. Since Tez started Hopdyke noticed the quality and prestige of his customers had improved immensely, as had his profits. Old bangers and cheap family run-arounds gave way to sports cars, luxury SUV's and the odd exotic. Never race cars, the street racers ignored the garage, having their own places hidden away. As the sun dipped behind the roof tops at last the guys in the garage, and the girls in the shop, got their superfluous coats and drifted away. Tez still worked on a Bentley Arnage he had been given that morning, a deep scratch from a key or a nail running down both flat green flanks. On the street outside the shop a small, red, tatty Vauxhall Corsa sat, engine idling. Waiting.

It was an hour since the others had left when Tez flipped the booth onto the right temperature to bake the Bentley's new paint. He dropped the roller shutters, set the alarm, and swung his leg over his bike. With an experienced eye he quickly checked the street before heading home. From the side of the road a small red car pulled out from a line of parked cars right in front of him. With nowhere to go Tez grabbed a fist full of front brake, locked both wheels and dropped the bike. Both man and machine slid briefly until they hit the plastic bumper. Tez was trying to work out what was him and what was bike when the car door opened and a shadow fell over him. Trapped under his bike Tez braced himself for the abuse car drivers usually gave when they cut up a bike. Instead the breath locked in his throat and he stared.

It started at the feet. Tanned lady's feet, with pink painted nails. Strange how a near death experience sharpens the sense, Tez thought randomly. The shoes were way too high to drive, but they shaped the long, smooth legs, a small scar on the left knee hidden under fake tan. The legs stopped high up, under a short, tight skirt. Not much there, and a small overhang of belly, complete with shining chain piercing. Up higher and past the expanse of exposed skin through a tight matching top a scared and upset, and very pretty face looked down.

"Oh my God, I'm so sorry! Are you alright?" She nearly cried the words out, her make up staying remarkably in place.

Tez lay, mouth still open, feeling like a bully had punched him in the gut. Bile, sour and horrid, threatened to rise. His face reddened and his Kevlar biker jeans became tighter on the crotch. His voice, however, had gone on holiday.

"You ok?" the girl asked again, tears starting to run. Tez was vaguely aware there were people crowding around, some hands reaching for the bike. His left leg felt heat, the exhaust. For all he cared the devil himself could be invading the world with his demonic hoard. This girl, with the sun lighting her pale blonde hair, those green eyes swimming in tears, had quite literally stolen his breath.

More hands turned up and the bike was lifted. Tez let them. He realised he was staring, glad he wore a full face helmet. To the girl his open, unmoving eyes looked like those of a corpse.

Tez sat up, did a quick self diagnostic, the report was a bruised hip, aching shoulder, numb but usable hand, and a pounding heart. Taking his helmet off he first saw the scrape on the side of it. Another scrapped lid to add to the collection. Next he saw the pretty girl squat down, knees together, to be level with his face. Her green eyes searched his hazel ones. He felt the spark, maybe she did too, as the tears stopped.

"Hi," said Tez, mumbling like a child on his first day at a new school.

"Hi." She smiled showing perfect teeth. Tez felt another wave of nausea and heat flow over him.

"Tez, err, Terrence." He held out his right hand, the inner voice screaming to stop being an ass. Confused the girl took it, shaking it gently.

"Christine," she said. "You wanna get up, Tez?"

"Probs a good idea." Groaning he rolled onto his hands and knees, slowly getting to his feet. Upright she stood a few inches lower, but still able to kiss without bending. Chasing the thoughts of lust away Tez nodded dumbly and checked his bike over. A bent lever, broken front indicator and a scuffed mirror showed it was a slow speed spill. He could ride it home. Christine followed him, ignoring the crowd, some volunteering their numbers to be a witness.

"Is it ok? Did I wreck it?" she asked, tears welling again.

"Nah," said Tez. "Just a bit bent. Easy fix."

"I want to pay, I have insurance, but name the price and I will pay it." She rummaged in her hand bag, taking out a pen and an old window envelope. She wrote on it hurriedly, tongue sticking out the corner of her mouth. This gave Tez another wave of feelings, making him sway slightly. Christine missed this, concentrating on her note. When she had finished she folded it, holding the note like it was a bank card in a shop. Tez took it, feeling the closeness.

"You sure you are ok?" she asked again, dry eyed, but

still worried.

"I'm fine, and seriously don't worry about paying. Got the stuff at home anyway. Just a matter of minutes to fix." He missed the fact his damaged helmet was nearly two weeks wages alone. No need to make her feel worse.

"Never the less, call me." She said it almost as a request, batting eyes and a trace of a pout. The waves came back with a vengeance, Tez had to hold onto his bike to support himself. She hesitated, then got back into her car and left. The crowd dispersed, the excitement over. Left alone Tez watched the empty road where the little red car had been, then pulled his helmet back on and went home.

It was getting dark, dusk making the shadows grow, when Tez parked under the steps of his flat. Running up the stairs he searched through the only decent cupboard for the parts, sliding nimbly down the metal rail of the steps to his bike. Half an hour, and near black, he finished changing the bent clutch lever, broken indicator, and straightened the bent gear selector on the foot peg. Back in his flat Tez took a pair of scissors and cut the straps from his helmet, and left it on the balcony. Taking a new one from the grey box he put it on and spent the rest of the night wearing it, feeling stupid, but knowing that was better than the ache a new helmet gave you on a bike. Exhausted he stripped and had a shower. Checking the new bruises on his left hip and leg, a smaller one on his elbow, he blasted hot water to sooth the aches, then lay naked on his bed to dry. Looking down he was still hard, that body fresh on his mind. Reaching for the TV remote Tez dealt with that last before falling into a happy sleep.

Every two weeks, on a Monday nights, the Black Bull pub closed early, not that there was ever any customers anyway. Only a select few would come, those with money in rolls in their pockets, or in envelopes. All the tables were cleaned, chairs upside down on top, save one. This had a green cloth covering it. Alvin laid out the multicoloured chips, two sealed decks of cards, and the drinks his guests would want. As he always did he hated himself. He knew he was an addict. But the only way out of the black pit of gambling was to win, and win he must. He was good at poker, having won a few trophies. That was before his wife, Christine's mother, had died. She could play a hand, and the fortnightly poker nights were her idea. Now only three turned up, and they were good. Alvin had toyed with the idea of dropping the nights, saying he had lost the taste for poker. It wasn't far from the truth, but only because he had also lost a lot of money. Christine knew he was in debt, but not by how much. He owned the Bull, but his debt to one player totalled half the pub's value.

Bang on 9pm the door creaked open and in came his poker group. The only main rival, the one who had the most chits, was Colin Hopwood. He came last, pockets bulging. He laid down three thick rolls of notes held tight with elastic bands. The other two had smaller rolls. Alvin had a thin stack from the till.

They sat around the table, counting one by one the cash they had. Maurice Peterson had a decent wad, totalling five thousand pounds. Doctor Frederic Pearson had less, only three grand. Colin had over ten. Alvin sheepishly counted his fifteen hundred, converting it to the relevant number of chips.

"Where's that pretty kid of yours?" the plump Maurice asked.

"Like you have a chance," smiled the lanky doctor.

"I don't know," said Alvin, making an effort to look around as if searching for her.

Colin stacked his high pile of chips, and said "Never

mind. We here to play cards, or look at pussy?"

Alvin opened his mouth to say his only daughter was not 'pussy' but decided against it. Maybe if Colin was left in a decent mood he could win back some of his debt.

"Hmm. I hope this ain't gonna be a dry game," mumbled
Maurice. "Need to keep my fluids up, ay doc?"

"You need to shed about three stone, lose the fatty carbs and hit the gym, old friend," replied Pearson.

Colin threw his head back and roared with laughter, shocking everyone. When he calmed down he smiled and threw in a £100 chip.

"We playing then?" he asked. Alvin held in a sigh, tore the plastic from the first deck, and shuffled. He only hoped tonight wouldn't ruin him. Where was that girl?

In the puddles of street lights outside his flat Tez had no idea of the trouble brewing. A soft, almost apologetic knock on his door slowly pulled him from sweet dreams. With an exasperated look at the digital display on the alarm clock he rolled out of bed, landing with a thump, and reached wildly for clothes. He'd slept an hour. Giving up on clothes, another knock more persistent he decided to give this disturbing caller a rude send off. Waddling in his boxers he crossed the now clear flat and unlocked the door. He nearly slammed it when he saw the figure on the other side.

"Hi," said Christine, blushing in the harsh lights.

"Err, hi," said Tez, hiding most of himself behind the door. He raised a single forefinger. "Just one second." He closed the door, now fully awake. Panicked he rushed around, pulling clothes out, sniffing them, dropping them and trying others. Finally he found some clean smelling jeans and a t-shirt. Still barefoot he opened the door.

Christine briefly checked out his new look, and smiled.

"Better?" she asked.

"Yeah, I guess," said Tez. "Wassup?"

Christine stared at his feet. "I just wanted to be sure you were ok, and to say sorry again."

"Oh." Tez tried to hide his disappointment. In his hurried clothes hunt he had let his mind fantasise about the pretty blonde coming to find him, wanting him. Like a porn movie they ended up naked, sweaty, screaming. He imagined waking the next morning, smelling like sex, her naked body next to his, her hair on his pillow, an arm over his chest.

"I was worried," Christine said, seeing his slight downcast look. "And to ask if you wanted to go for something to eat sometime. I feel I owe it to you." She nearly blurted the words out, falling over themselves to be said. "And I can't afford a claim on my insurance you see, my dad will kill me when he sees the scratch. Already in crap for the rest of the car. If I say I hit a biker he'd go spare. I wanna make sure you are happy."

Tez held back the relief, trying to appear indifferent. "You wanna make sure I don't sue you?"

"Yeah, and I kinda hoped you'd come out with me."

"Like a date?"

Christine looked up, half shock, half hope. "I suppose, if you wanted to call it that."

Tez held her gaze, searching her eyes. She seemed uncomfortable, but there was something more than an apology there. She felt more than fear of a compensation claim. She felt something.

"I'm free Saturday night," Tez said eventually, still leaning on the door frame as casually as he could manage. "Saturday? Perfect. Say seven?"

Tez looked up, pretending he was thinking. "Can't

remember anything on then. That'll do for me. Seven it is."

Christine half giggled and said "seven it is. I'll pay for the meal."

"Don't make me much of a gentleman if I let the lady pay," Tez said with false pride.

"Don't make me much of a driver if I can't see a motorbike," Christine replied.

Tez laughed and she joined in, tension melting like spring snow. "Seven on Saturday. I'll even shave," he said, rubbing his stubble.

"Me too," said Christine and they both laughed again. She felt some warmth from this man, a warmth she didn't expect. Tez felt it too as they kept their eyes locked long after the laugh had passed. Discomfort set in, both knowing it had gone on too long.

"So, seven," said Tez.

"Seven," confirmed Christine. She found it hard to leave, like gravity was three times heavier. Tez felt weak, his knees threatening to give way.

"Seven," he said stupidly.

"Seven," she replied again. They both started laughing again. It felt like the old high school romance phone calls. You hang up, no you hang up.

"Bye then," Tez said, slowly closing the door.

"Bye," said Christine, actually leaning so she could still see him as the door swung shut. Once the latch had clicked she bent double, as if in pain, muttering 'stupid, stupid, stupid' under her breath. On the other side Tez leant on the closed door, hands in his head, his face on fire.

6

In the Bull the game was nearly over. After two hours Colin had won a lot, but was now losing to Maurice, who had a decent pile of everyone's chips. Alvin had done well to start with, making maybe three thousand at one point. But as much as he wanted to pull out there and then he couldn't, and now had half his original 1500 in front of him. The doctor was losing badly too, now sullen and complaining about everything.

"Bleeding weather here is crap. Too damn hot. Ain't you got air con in this dive, Al?" he moaned.

Maurice, who was easily double his weight, laughed. "You feel the heat, skinny git?"

"I do. Finely attuned to the environment. As a medical professional I need to be able to deduce more from my patient's problems than they say in words."

"Like a vet?" asked Colin. Maurice nearly fell of his chair, red faced. Pearson gave him a nasty look, and threw three £100 chips into the pile.

Alvin watched with fear and fascination. He had a decent hand, three of a kind, and maybe a straight if he got that last ace. He threw all his chips in.

"Call," he said.

Maurice looked at his cards, tears running down his face, and dropped them on the green felt. Pearson fingered his chips, then added another four. Colin watched with an experienced eye, saw the slight tremor in Alvin's cheek, and threw seven chips in.

Alvin spread his cards. "Three aces, and a queen," he said.

Pearson threw his down with more force than needed.

"Bleeding pair," was all he said.

Alvin looked at Colin, fear draining his face like an emptying bath. He was smiling, like the cat with the cream.

"Well, Alvin, seems we have an interesting result. I had most of a flush, but you beat me to it. Well played, for once." He dropped his cards and leant back. The bar clock chimed eleven, and as if on cue, Christie came in.

"Where the hell have you been?" Alvin yelled.

Colin sat up, eyes fixed.

"I went out," she said. "You gentlemen want a refill?"

"I think it's time we left," said Colin. "Thanks for the offer, but it's late. Same time in two weeks, chaps?" He stood, gathering his chips.

"Bleeding me dry tonight anyway," mumbled the doctor, scooping his chips into a neater pile. Maurice nodded, counting his stash. Once everyone was done they left. Christine locked and bolted the door while Alvin counted his winnings. He had actually made a big profit on that last hand, over three thousand pounds. He saw her head to the stairs out the corner of his eye.

"Where did you go?" he asked.

"Nowhere, just had to check a couple of things," she said, dismissing it.

"At eleven at night?"

"Yep."

Alvin put the cash in the till, too tired to bother with the safe. "Where?"

"Where?" asked Christine, wiping a beer tap.

"That's what I said. Where?"

"Nowhere. Just town."

"Town? There's no buses. How did you get there, hitch?"

She smiled, but his face was not responding. She

dropped the smile.

"Drove," she said, turning to go. He caught her shoulder, turning her back.

"Drove? You ain't got a car."

"I was given one."

"By who? Who the hell would give us a car?"

"Daddy, I was given it by Colin, if you must know. He said he worried about me being out late by myself."

"Not surprised dressed like a hooker," Alvin seemed placated, but still angry. "How can you afford it?"

"I'm not a hooker dad, it's called fashion."

"For hookers."

She gave a dramatic sigh. "He wants me to be safe. As my father I'd think you felt the same."

"I do," he said, calmer. "But I know that man, I knew him as a babby, I saw him grow up, his, his anger. I worry for you, more from him then anyone else. You push off the punters in here every night. You have a lot of your mother in you, maybe too much. You can take care of yourself, I know
I haven't done as well as I should."

She put her hand gently on his arm. "You did me proud, Dad. I know it was hard after mum died. Sorry if I upset you."

He shrugged her off, waving a hand. "You? Never. My little princess can never upset me," he smiled. It was a weak, uncertain smile. She did the same in return.

"Thanks, Dad." She turned and headed for the stairs. As she passed the door leading out of the bar she paused, looking over her shoulder. "I love you."

"Love you too, princess."

She smiled, a real one, and left. Feeling more wretched Alvin flicked a towel at the beer taps, poured himself a pint and sat in the empty bar. Before the cloudy beer settled he was crying.

The week passed quickly for everyone except Tez. He threw himself into his work, trying his best to fill the day and pass the time. He polished cars that didn't need it, swept clean floors, washed clear windows. He even went into the shop, annoying the girls there, sorting loose shelves, restocking full racks and fussing around customers. In his mind's eye he saw the pretty blonde standing over him still. When he wiped the white polish off a car's paintwork he saw her face staring back. On each box he moved, was her smile, on every poster, her body. He kept one eye on the yard, just in case. She knew where he lived, so she must know where he worked. She never showed. The guys teased him, his imaginary girlfriend. He ignored them until his patience wore thin, slamming one guy up against the wall until he apologised. Saturday dragged itself creaking and clanking around, the hands on the big white wall clock in the paint booth moved slowly around the plain face. The sun showed the same lethargy.

When half twelve finally came Tez nearly threw everyone out, even chasing a customer out the shop with parts still in hand unpaid. He had just a little over six hours to be ready. He rode home much too fast, almost jumping off the bike before he stopped, nearly forgetting the side stand. After cursing his enthusiasm, and saving the bike from landing on his leg a second time, he calmed himself and got organised. The little barber's shop was a five minute walk and that was his first stop. After a neat head shave, number three on top, two on the sides, he stopped at the corner shop for a new razor and shave gel. A short dash to the florists and he was paralysed by indecision.

"Which would you suggest for a young lady on a first date?" he asked the sour faced florist.

"Does she like anything in particular?" she asked, eyeing his scruffy clothes.

"I don't know. It's a first date."

With a barely noticeable roll of the eyes the florist swished by, heading for the most expensive she had. The young upstart would pay in cash for his attitude.

"If you wish to impress the young, hmm, lady, I would suggest roses. Always a firm favourite, and the most classic. A bunch of ten would seem fitting, and have a touch of class."

Tez saw the price per rose, but swallowed the protest before it got him into trouble. "Can you wrap them, please?"

"Certainly, sir." She plucked the worst ten and gave them a quick, but proper, trim and wrap. She still had her pride, even if the youth did not. After putting a large dent into his bank card Tez rushed home, unhappily aware it was gone four.

In his flat he washed the clothes he wanted to wear, and got out the polish. A few air fresheners and the flat was good enough. He put the clothes in the dryer and showered. Pulling the iron from the back of the closet he filled the dry chamber with water and put the best creases he could manage into the shirt, thinking of doing the jeans, then deciding against it. At 6:48 he slapped some aftershave on and studied himself in the wardrobe's big mirror. He looked half decent, but still not right. At exactly seven the a soft tap on the door made him jump. Taking deep breaths he opened it, and nearly choked. Christine stood in high heels, the tightest pair of jeans ever, a short top showing the shape of her breasts, no bra, and a little jacket.

"Hi," Tez croaked.

"Hi back," she smiled.

"So, err, where are we going?"

"The little Italian just outside town, good?"

"Sure." Tez loved Italian food. He grabbed his door keys and locked up. On the roadside he looked up and down the empty street. "Where's your car?"

"Car?" She looked puzzled, then alarmed. "Oh, sorry. It' broke down. Old piece of crap."

"Ah. I don't have a spare helmet or we could take bike."

"Don't you have a car?" she asked, almost childlike.

"Yeah, but I don't use it often."

"Beats walking," she said.

Tez shrugged, and reluctantly got the keys from his flat. opening the garage Christine gasped at the race car.

"Lucky I have a second seat," Tez joked. He helped her in, the tightness of her jeans and the heels making it hard in more ways than one. With a check of her four point harness, face close to hers, smelling her perfume, seeing the rise and fall of her chest, Tez got in the drivers seat and turned the key, letting the engine warm to a settled idle. With a deep breath he put it into gear and drove off. Just around the corner, by another set of garages, a figure watched them go, then got into the red Corsa and drove after them.

7

La Famiglia lay out in the country, past the town limits. Run by the Laverti brothers since it opened thirty years before, it stayed a family run affair, serving traditional Italian cuisine. Ricky Laverti would never call himself snobbish, or a prude, but the nicely dressed young man who came in that Saturday night stank of ban news and cologne. The girl with him could have been on a pay per view adult channel if her clothes and make up were anything to go by. They fitted as well with the other diners as a call girl and a pimp at the Ritz. Still, they had money, and evidently taste in food, so Ricky ignored his gut feelings and lead them to a table, albeit a small one hidden in a corner out the way. A wicker weave screen helped keep them out of sight. For Tez it was perfect, almost intimate. For Christine it felt like a jail cell, but in the best prison in the world. They sat, he ordered wine for her, and a Pepsi for himself. Left alone they looked absently at the menu, mostly in Italian with English translations underneath.

Christine lay her menu down on the table, over the decorative napkin folded like a fan. "I can't choose. It all looks too nice, and strange."

Tez smiled. When Ricky came over Tez referred briefly to the menu, speaking smooth common Italian, ordering starter and main for both of them. Impressed, and surprised, Ricky bowed politely, deciding to knock a little off the bill for the nicely spoken young man with the questionably dressed lady friend. Christine stared open mouthed.

"I learn languages easily," Tez explained.

"So I see. You speak anything else?"

"German, Russian, a little English." Tez laughed. So did Christine.

"You from any of those places originally?" she asked.

"Nah. Born north of here, small place near Derby. Live the same place all my life until uni."

"You got a degree?"

Tez shook his head, a moment of doubt darkening his

face. "Long story."

"I'm not rushing anywhere." She gave her sweet, girlfriend smile, the one that always got the big tips in the pub.

Tez sighed, pouring some water from the jug on the table into their glasses. After draining half of his glass he fixed her a look, almost of pain. She wished she could suck the words back in.

"I tried hard, but the financial, business world out there sucks big time. You tried dealing with big companies?" She shook her head.

"Don't. Ever. Gave them a real money maker. Could have made them millions. Instead they said it was 'too experimental'. Said it couldn't make them money without extensive investment. Posh talk for 'sod off, we don't care'.
None of them even offered me a job in development."

"What did you study?"

"Motor Racing, degree level. Was already applying to race teams after my first year. Five year course. By year three I found most teams won't hire without experience. How the hell can you get experience without doing the job?"

Christine kept silent, feeling the pain and frustration. Tez kept his voice low, but the venom in his words screamed.

"So I gave in. My dad had money. Not a lot, but enough. Make our own team, we decided. We got an old ST Fiesta and tuned the nuts off it. Went for the small car cup, was gonna win too. But I blew the engine half way through the season. Had no cash to replace, so sold the lot. Back to the drawing board."

Tez paused as one of the waiters put their drinks down. When they were alone again he resumed.

"So I went back to uni after the summer break was over, spoke to some of the egg heads in the science labs. Had a massive metallurgy department, and some real boffins there. I worked out a plan to reshape the combustion chamber of the head, and the shape of the piston crown. With a few little tweaks it could burn 70% better, I thought. So I spoke to the guys. They laughed, so I kept talking. Slowly they stopped laughing, then got the whiteboard markers out. Turns out I was right. Not only that, but I figured the near perfect design from the start. Then disaster."

Christine cupped the wine in her hands, eyes open, mouth closed.

"Found the engine couldn't take the heat, or the strain. Test models went bang quite impressively." Tez smiled at a memory, quickly fading. "So it was back to the board again. I searched through other options. Nothing could take that heat and the pressures. The boffins drew blanks too. It was the following summer, when my dad's old Vauxhall blew the head gasket I figured it. That burnt and bent metal wafer, blackened in the middle, made me think of carbon, and steel. Not like they do now, mixed together, but as a composite material. Steel lined cylinders, with a carbon block, and steel supports. Small scale was amazing. We managed to drive a car with an engine that was smaller than a shoe box. Took it to every car maker in the country. They all rejected it. Small scale was fine, but not a real, working car with the strains of daily use." Tez drained his water, refilled the glass, and looked into the clear liquid as if seeing the future, or the past, in the curved glass.

"So we made a full sized version. Was easy enough. Found a strong car to fit it, one with a gearbox to take the power. We had no idea what it would produce, so we moulded it in the lab, and cleaned it up in the workshop. Final thing was less than fifty kilos. Could pick it up by yourself. We tested it on the small service road out the back of the uni. Nearly hit the wall at the end. The road is half a mile long. Damn thing flew. So we took it to a dyno to see the power. That twelve hundred cc engine made three hundred horsepower. Three bleeding hundred. So we made another, a 1.5 litre. With a better gearbox and suspension upgrades, and the biggest brakes we could get. The thing ended up with 600 BHP. My dad found out about it, and suggested a track day. Always a laugh, my dad. So we did. That old car thrashed super cars, exotics, tuners, even the bloody bikes. Ran like it was a scalextric car."

"That the car outside?" Christine asked, breaking her silence, wine untouched and now warm.

"Yeah. Smoked every car in Derbyshire. My guys would put feelers out for punters. Put down the cash, or the log book, and race. We made a mint."

"I'll bet. And you made it yourself?"

"Yep. That's how I got my name." "I did wonder," said Christine.

"The fourth Fast and Furious film had come out, and the guy on there called Tej was a genius on it, so they called me Tez."

Christine giggled. "Thought it was strange, seeing how Terrence is usually Terry or Tel."

"Yep. Anyhoo I won myself quite a reputation."

The waiter came back with starters, a strange soup with ciabatta bread drizzled in olive oil. It smelt amazing and both fell silent again as they tucked in. Tez noticed she tried to eat like the other women there, prim and proper. He just dived in, spoon held like a child, elbows out wide. When the bowls were wiped clean with the bread

Christine dabbed the corners of her mouth with her napkin, leaving pink lipstick stains. Tez belched quietly, making her giggle. She had an infectious laugh, and soon Tez was laughing with her.

"Sorry," he said, holding a hand up and belched again.

"Don't be. I'm having a great time," she replied. Suddenly she reached out and took his hand, holding it between her own. He put his other hand on top, caught in her affection. Ricky saw this from across the restaurant and smiled. The nice young man had finally made the move on his new lady friend he thought, and asked the table he was serving for their order.

Tez was dumbstruck. All words dried in his throat. His heart felt like it would pound through his chest, making a heart shaped lump in his shirt like a cartoon character. If she pouted and fluttered her long eyelashes his eyes would probably shoot out on stalks, his tongue unroll like a carpet.

Her hands felt cold, and dry. Her face showed something he hadn't seen, or felt, in years. Affection. True, real, unhidden affection. His jeans grew tight around his crotch.

The waiter coughed. They both started, realising they were blocking the table, and the man laid two plates of pasta and chicken down a little more forcefully then needed. Pasta polished off, Tez dropped his napkin over the plate. Christine struggled, but managed to eat it all, and leant over her plate, elbows on the table, chin in her hands. Tez saw her pretty face like a bust of some ancient goddess. The plinth the bust was mounted on was also impressive. Her chest in the tight top still rose and fell gently, sexually. Her tanned belly creased like ripples, the jeans digging into her waist. His crotch tightened again.

"Then what happened," she asked, her wine half drunk.

"Happened?"

"With your reputation."

"Ah, yes. Well I won a lot, made a lot, and wasted a lot. When you have wads in the bum pocket people seem to queue up to help it go. Drugs, women, drink, you name it, I dabbled in it. Got stupid after a while. I never did hard stuff, mostly uppers and some brown pills, you know? The others did coke, a lot of weed, and base. That got them. The driving got serious too. We raced even when there was nobody to race. One guy got creamed by a lorry and the rozzers came down hard on us. Drugs bust, drink driving, illegal mods on the cars. None of it stuck luckily. We had enough bad stuff to get a caution, nothing more. The coppers almost screamed at the judge. I ended up with a year suspended sentence for reckless driving. After another got creamed in a race I dropped out."

"Dropped out?"

Tez leant back, staring at the ceiling. He spoke soft, quiet.

"I saw the future. I saw my death, my end. I knew it was going that way. I'd ruined them guys. We had fun, but it went to my head, and their veins. One day you wake up in a grotty flat surrounded by hookers, drugs and empty beer cans. You see a mate from school with a needle in his arm asleep, or dead, who can tell? I did it, not them." Tez dropped his head, pain, even tears in his eyes. "So I left. Took the cash I had, plenty left hidden from the raid, left a note explaining, texted them all and left. Threw my phone in a bin outside town and never looked back. Drifted here, found a job, a new life."

"You miss it?" Christine breathed.

"Miss it? Sure as shit. No feeling like racing, like beating the pants off some smug ass hole who talks crap. No feeling like having a fat roll of cash in your jeans and nothing to worry about. But it don't last long. You either end up dead, or in a concrete box with bars for doors. Not worth it."

"You thought about going legit? You got a race car, so race it. Make your living that way."

Tez shook his head. He avoided her gaze, making her move herself to try to see his face.

"Won't work. Too many rules. You live by your own code when you race the streets. I'd be thrown off the track after the warm up lap."

Christine sipped her wine, face full of trouble. The night had taken a bad turn for her.

"Anyway," said Tez, trying to brighten the mood. "What about you?"

"Sod all to say really," Christine said, brushing hair from her face with a manicured hand.

"Must be something."

"Nope. Tried school, tried hard, but my mum died and that threw me."

"Sorry to hear that," Tez said automatically.

"Thanks. My dad tried, but he can't be a mum too."

"True. No tits."

Christine laughed so suddenly Tez almost thought she was choking.

"Yeah, no tits. But I got them early. Found the boys, even the teachers, could be manipulated. Like the old song said, I got legs, I knew how to use them."

"ZZ Top," Tez said.

"Yeah. Three points. Hear a lot of old cheese in work."

"Classic song. Where do you work?"

Christine looked away. "I don't, right now. Hoping to go to college, probably too late."

"Never too late," said Tez. Sensing it was a touchy subject he changed it quickly. "You fancy pud? Got a nice sundae on the menu."

"I couldn't eat if my life depended on it," she said.

"Me neither. Gonna need a wheelbarrow to get me out of here."

"You still look good for a man who over ate," she said, blushing.

"I doubt that," Tez replied.

"Well you look better than me. I'm really getting frumpy."

"You look amazing, beautiful." Tez tried to stop the last word, and failed. Her eyes fired up to his, searching for a lie, a joke. There was none. The air around them felt heavy, like a thunderstorm. Christine feared her hair would frizz.

"Why don't I go pay the bill, before we eat ourselves stupid?" he said, not really asking, already standing. Christine nodded to his back, lowered her head, and cursed silently. Tez walked quickly to the bar, face flushed, feeling an idiot. Ricky saw this and got to the till first.

"Everything ok, sir?" he asked.

Tez nodded. "Delicious. Can I have the bill, please?"

"Certainly, sir." Ricky moved fast, feeling the poor young man's night hadn't gone the way he had hoped. Maybe a botched proposal? Too early in their relationship, so must be a compatibility issue. He passed the slip over on a small plastic tray, the bottom edge folded to hide the total. Tez barely read it, handing his bank card over. He didn't look to Christine, who downed her wine, wishing it was something stronger. Bill paid Tez thanked Ricky for a wonderful meal, promising to come again. Ricky doubted it would be with the same lady. Good thing too. She was too trashy for him.

Without a word Tez went back to the table, finished his

cola and looked to his date. Christine, flushed with the wine, smiled weakly and stood, trying to pull her small jacket down to cover her exposed midriff. In the car park Tez opened her door for her, receiving a smile as thanks. He never noticed the fingerprints around the car, or the marks on the drivers door lock. As the Volvo pulled out onto the dark road the small red car followed.

Back at his flat Tez sat in the car, letting the carbon race engine idle, cool. Christine had kept her silence all the way back.

"You sure you don't want a lift home?" Tez asked.

"I'm fine, thanks. I don't live far, and I grew up here. I know the bad places."

"Ok." Tez wasn't happy her walking alone, almost making his mind up to follow her, but that felt like stalking and he didn't want this to go any worse tonight.

They both sat staring at the puddles of light spaced regularly down the street. Finally Christine undid her harness.

"Well, thank you, Tez, for an enjoyable night."

"You're welcome. Sorry I was a bore."

"No, I enjoyed it." She opened the door, letting the night cool in. Hesitating she leant over and kissed his cheek.

"Same time next week?"

"Err, yeah, sure. I mean, of course. I would love to." Tez babbled as his face glowed.

Christine laughed, got out and left. Needing to clear his head Tez put the car in first and when her tight jeans had wiggled around the corner out of sight, he headed for the hills.

She waited for the sound of his car to fade, relieved he had left quickly. She saw the car parked down the road, lights off, engine running. She got in, the courtesy light stayed off.

"Well done, love," said the driver. He opened his door, leaving the car running. Leaning through into the car he said "tell your old man he just shaved a tenth off." The man shut the door, leaving her in the passenger seat. Unable to hold it back Christine dropped her head into her hands and cried.

Tez didn't know it, nor did Ricky for that matter, but had anyone seen the CCTV screen for the car park they would have seen in the ghostly green and grey image a small car park past all the others. A man in a hoodie got out, moving purposefully to the race car parked under the camera. The man took what looked like keys from his pocket, but spent too long at the lock before the door opened. Ducking inside he pulled the bonnet release, then locked the door again. Opening the bonnet the man spent five minutes looking around the engine, before closing it softly but firmly. He then walked around the car twice, looking underneath with a pen light. With a last look under the rear the man stood and went back to his small car just out of camera shot.

8

Inspector Henderson felt the heaviness of the air, although not thunder he knew lightning was coming, and fireworks. Knowing without proof his hands were tied, he reached out to his contacts, his moles. One rolled into the empty lay-by off the near deserted dual carriageway. The Range Rover sat big and broody, towering over the small Mazda RX8 like a stallion standing beside a pony. Henderson already had his window open, and when the little car was alongside the tinted glass on the passenger side slid down.

"You got something?" Henderson asked.

"Maybe. You got something?" the voice in the dark answered.

Henderson took a thin envelope from the big cubby box between the front seats. He folded it, and dropped it into the passenger seat of the Mazda. A hand took it, tearing of paper coming on the warm breeze. The interior light came on, the lowered car kept the driver hidden, not that Henderson didn't know who it was. After less than a minute the light went out.

"Word is Colin has found something, a car that can beat anything," the voice said.

"A car? His? Someone he knows? I need more than that."

"I got more." The voice sounded irritated, but also scared.

He was taking a big risk. "Word is the car belongs to a new kid, works at Hopdyke's place."

"I know the guy. Rides a bike."

"That's him. Keeps it hidden in a lock up, races the hills alone at night. Called Taz or something."

Henderson nodded. He knew most of this already, but confirmation was a very good thing.

"What is Colin doing about it?"

"He's got a plan, gonna lure the kid in, and take it from him, all legal like."

"Will it?"

The other car gave a non committal grunt. "Maybe. He don't wanna hurt him, or he loses the secret of how it all works. Think he wants this kid on his side."

"Does his brother know?"

"Not by me, or anyone else. Maybe, but not the details.

The car has been seen by a few, and word spreads."

"Yes, it does." Henderson pondered the news. "Well done. Let me know if anything else comes up."

"I will next time a speeding fine turns up." The driver laughed, closing his window and roared off. Henderson sat in silence, radio off, and thought. So the new kid was in it deep, and the poor sod didn't even know. Now to do some classic police surveillance. Keying the big V8 Henderson followed the Mazda, turning for home as the small car headed south into town.

Tez opened the garage Monday morning as normal. Nothing seemed out of place that day. The warm spring still promised to turn slowly into a hot summer. The thin clouds were tinted a mild gold as the sun rose. Tez punched in the alarm code, cutting the beeping off, rolled all the shutters up, and let the fresh air drift in. Dust, oil, strange chemical smells all rolled out, like a shift change. The dew clung to the stunted tufts of grass in the concrete yard and slowly dried, letting the blades rise to face the day.

The other mechanics came in spread out, some purposeful, some lazy. They didn't clock in or out like the air, but they did have to beat old man Hopdyke. The sharp edge of his temper was not to be risked. The jokes started as soon as the kettle rocked on the wobbly desk. Banter, games, some dirty stories and false claims filled the high, old garage. Tez let it surround him, wrapped like a blanket. It was warm with fond memories, and comforting. The hint of sadness was there, but smaller now. He knew he could join in, let down his defences, but he had seen enough friends hurt. He didn't want to make new ones, to just do the same. Making his own tea from a smaller kettle by his paint booth Tez paused, troubled. He had made a new friend, someone who was beginning to mean a lot to him. Christine. She seemed a decent lass, one who had some past, he had no doubt on that. But someone who had a future too, whether she knew it or not. There was fire in that girl, a flame focused, blue and powerful. If she found her true calling there would be no stopping her. But could he be the brakes to her life? He shunned friends for their safety, yet he was falling for this girl with the green eyes over her little nose stud, the round, firm chest framing that smooth, tanned belly.

He shook his head, trying to rid the image from his mind's eye. Dropping a tea bag into his mug, Tez waited for his kettle and thought. As always his eyes landed on his bike. He'd always liked motorbikes, and a CBR was a tough old cookie. Even the 600cc could move well enough. For him it meant freedom to get out, feel the breeze, smell the country air, and pound the tarmac. It was also small, light, easy to hide and fast enough to get him out of town. Sadly Tez realised he had made this new life to be disposable, to be jettisoned at a moments notice. Christine was becoming the only anchor.

He had known plenty of women before he fled. Some were groupies wanting to share the glory, paying with their bodies like all good gold diggers. Tez used them the way they wanted, but never felt satisfied. Some, a small few, were more to him. They shared him like a good book, enjoying what he had to offer, but making sure they did him no harm. He liked that. There was no guilt, no deceit, no shame. If one had him, they sorted between themselves, or shared at the same time. Those were the best times. A mixing bowl of arms, legs, buttocks, heads and other parts all moving over each other, moaning, breathing, wanting. They were good times, the memory bringing a smile to his face as he poured the hot water. They were the good days. Then came the drugs, the fights, the law. That night when the raid came, three vans full of armed police. They took the door clean off it's hinges. Tez was in bed with three girls when they dragged him out. They were all lined up, naked and angry, against a wall. The house was turned over, drugs, money, weapons all piled on the table in the dining room. The dream, that had gone from his university dorm, through his parents house, to a four bedroom semi in a decent part of town, had crashed. With no money to pay the rent the house went. The guys tried to rally back, winning races, winning cash, and buying a flat. But the police raided that, found more of the same, and threw the book. Tez was out that night. Lucky, or he would have been released from her majesty's pleasure a couple of months ago, like the others. The empty flat screamed at him, scaring him off. He ran. And he never looked back. To go home would put him in jail. He wasn't arrested, nor was a warrant issued, but if he went back they could tie him in so he left that night.

And now it could happen again. Friends were powerful tools. They made you happy when you are down, cheered you when you win, consoled you when you lose. They are family, but a family you can hurt, can drag down. Tez had done that once. Never again. Nobody deserved the pain he had caused, the lives he had ruined. He couldn't repair the damage, but he could lessen the effect. He could keep away.

Sipping the hot tea, feeling the cool morning breeze slowly warm as well Tez idly thought over Christine, the work for today, his lunch. He hardly heard the bike engine until it rumbled through the alley leading to the yard. By then it had him pinned.

It was a dark green Kawasaki, the newer H2R, Tez had read about them, but never seen one. Rare, and stupidly powerful, they put even exotic sports cars to shame. The supercharged 1000cc engine was the key, the mighty heart that moved itself with nearly 300 thoroughbred horses. The owner of a bike like that didn't stop by back street garages.

The rider, a fairly tall man in skin tight leathers, pulled off his helmet, Arai, Tez noticed, and looked right at him. Jacked unzipped, trousers creaking he hobbled in paddock boots past Tez, and crouched by his Honda. Uncertain, Tez coughed, tea still in hand.

"Yeah?" asked the man, creaking upright.

"Who the fuck are you?" Tez asked.

"Mark," said the man, without holding out his hand, or even turning to face Tez.

"Ok, Mark. Now what do you want?" Tez was beginning to feel the burn of annoyance. Who was this guy?

Mark turned and smiled. Strangely the anger died as if the smile were a fire extinguisher.

"Terrence, right?" he asked.

"Yeah," Tez replied, guarded.

"Good. Heard there was a guy here with an old CBR. Good old thing, eh? Had one years ago. Loved the throttle response"

Tez tried to hate this random stranger, but his voice, the blue eyes, the dark ponytail, all made his negative vibes fall away. Something remained, a rotten under smell, like a cleaned shirt that still had the odour of what it once was covered in.

"Yeah, it is good. What's it to you?"

Mark kept the smile, unmoving, one hand on the bars, other hanging by his hip. "You ride much?"

"Everyday, to work and back."

"Not got a car?"

Tez fixed him a stare. "Yeah. And?"

"Nice weather for riding. Can't fault you for using it. You ever raced?"

Tez said nothing, mind racing to find the reason for this abstract talk, to get ahead of the game.

Mark still smiled. "You ever raced?" he asked again.

"Look, Mark. I ain't got a clue what you want, but I got stuff to do, and the gaffer will be here soon. So if you got something to say, say it."

The smile dropped, almost making Tez flinch. Mark left go of the bar, creaking his way to stand in front of Tez. Bracing himself in case this leather clad biker swung, Tez stared him down. Around them the garage fell silent. Seeing the rare bike in the yard the others, too early for the shop girls to be here, had gathered to see the bike, and saw the stand off. Tez and Mark were oblivious to it all, seeing only each other, squaring off. After a moment Mark suddenly smiled, tension gone.

"You are one tough git," he said, still looking at Tez. "Fair play. You also ain't stupid. You got a race car, right? Silver and black? Fast as hell."

"Yeah," said Tez, still trying to think ahead.

"And you have raced the hills alone?"

"Yeah."

"And you know of the 4power group?

Tez felt like a broken record. "Yeah," was all he managed.

Mark leant closer, dropping his voice. "I know they came to see you, kid with a purple Evo. What did he say? Did he try to recruit you?"

Realisation dawned like the sun above him, slow, but showing all clearly. He held in a laugh of relief.

"The kid had scuffed his car. He wanted it fixing. He never said anything about joining."

Mark kept his face plain. "So you didn't turn him down?"

"Nope. He never asked for anything other than a repair job. I gave him that."

Mark searched his face for a hint of a lie. "So why did they kick him out? Why was he forced to leave town, if not for failure?"

Tez blinked, the expression saying more than words ever could. Mark realised the man who stood before him was telling the truth.

"So you really ain't joining the power boys?" Mark asked.

"I don't want to join anyone, just live in peace." Tez felt the irritation begin to boil again.

"Good. You won't hear from us, but I doubt they will ever leave you alone." Mark zipped his jacket up, creaked to his bike and swung a stiff leg over. Looking at Tez he pulled his lid on, flicked up the kick stand and thumbed the starter. As Mark turned the small bike around Tez caught the Japanese lettering on the leathers, and the styled words 'Yoki' on the back. Feeling more worried then ever Tez drained his tea and went to check on his bike, just in case.

As he gave it a glance over a shadow darkened his view. Half turning he saw it was the boss, half bent with his back, looking at him with a look of deep suspicion.

"What did he want?" he asked.

"Nothing, Mr Hopdyke, just some random questions about my bike."

"Some questions. Hmm." For a man nearing 70, Henry Hopdyke looked like a doddering old man, but inside was a power like a wizard. "Son, do you know who that was?"

"Mark, he said," Tez replied.

"Follow," said Hopdyke, shuffling away.

Flicking the booth heater off, Tez followed, knowing the old man wasn't a fast walker. He caught him halfway across the yard, headed for the back of the shop. Inside the back room Hopdyke led through the storeroom, down narrow aisles of dusty car parts and promotional posters. Metal racking ended at the small canteen, a tiny room with three tables and a bad smell of stale food. Pausing to kick a table back into place the old man resumed his shuffle, opening his office door and going in. Without a word he lowered himself gently into the padded recliner, caught his breath, and looked to Tez.

"Sit," he said as if to a dog. Tez sat in the ripped metal framed chair facing the desk. On the wall years of dirty calendars showing topless girls, some now in their fifties, posters from parts suppliers, and the big clock stared down on him. Hopdyke watched the man he had hired on a hunch, one that hadn't proved him wrong yet. The cloud that had hung over the man was still there, but it was growing now. The change was coming on stronger.

"Mark Hopwood, young man, is the better half of a pair of pieces of crap. I knew their old mum, a decent girl with a nice ass and great tits. She knew how to handle your meat too, if you follow." He didn't wait for an answer. "She met a drifter, but a good one, like you, and married him. Settled down her wild streak, and she could streak." The old face warmed briefly, wrinkles fading as if time was reversing. "She had two boys and a girl. The little girl was the best. She kept them apart. She was the oldest by a year on Mark. She stopped the fights, sorted the disputes, like the UN she kept the peace. Lasted until she was 19."

Hopdyke paused long enough to pull a bottle from the top desk drawer, twist the cap off and take a slug. He left the unmarked brown bottle on the cluttered desk top, uncapped.

"Anyway, she had just passed her test, drove a safe little runner. Just down the road, before the bypass was built. One nice sunny day she was off to meet friends. Never made it. Found her car half embedded in a tree. Police said someone ran her off the road, but they never found out who. That was the end of the peace. Those two boys fought worse than before, ended up spilling onto the streets. Mark, being the older of the two, had his biker buddies first. He's not too bad a guy, wicked temper but he controls it. A bit too smart for his own good maybe. He can inspire loyalty from the devil himself. His brother, Colin, is the real piece of crap. Anger rules him, and his own. His poor ma, God rest her soul, died of a broken heart six years past. Their da vanished after that, couldn't handle them. Apart they are manageable. Together, it's like two jump leads, big sparks. Colin races cars, another thing they fight over. That started the war."

Tez sat in silence, the story filling his ears with wonder, and his heart with dread. The gravity in the room seemed to treble, the air like soup. The regular thump of his heart throbbed in his ears, filling his throat.

"So, they fought like kids," Hopdyke resumed. "They fought, their friends fought. Main street became a war zone. They raced all over the place, in town, in the hills, anywhere. Coppers couldn't stop them, even the town couldn't stop them. Got to the point folks got hurt. Three died when a race hit town on market day. One poor sod out there lost his family. After that the reality bit them. Mark spoke to his brother for the first time in years. A truce was called. They still fight, but they do it on the airstrip south of here. Every year they meet, every year they race. Winner takes all. The last is the big one, brother against brother. So far they haven't won, either of them. A dead draw. Mark is ok with that. Think he likes it. Colin isn't. For him it's all or nothing. Not having all the town eats him. Every year he's gotten more desperate, more ambitious. He hurts people if they don't give him what he wants." Hopdyke leant forwards, pain from his back creasing his face. Eyes fixed on Tez he spoke slowly. "He will either take you, or break you if he thinks you have something he wants. Make sure you don't."

Tez tried to swallow, and gave up. Fear had dried his throat. He knew there was some history here, you can't hide something like that. Town was small but not that small. The depth of the truth had shocked him.

Hopdyke saw his words had sunken in. Leaning back he waved a hand. "I ain't paying you to sit there with your mouth open. Go earn your keep."

Dismissed Tez walked numbly back to the booth. He felt as if he had dropped into a deep well, and the water was rising. The worse part was he didn't know what to do, or even if he should. One thing to do that day was to move the car. Fast.

9

Monday night held the warmth of the day, most people leaving windows open. As the street lights glowed like fireflies a figure slipped around the flats and stopped by one of the garage doors. With a bar he levered the locks off one by one. Prising the door open a shrill alarm sounded, making dogs bark and windows light up as residents looked out. The figure ignored them, lifting the metal door fully, then running into the night.

A small crowd had gathered by the door when Tez came down. Some wanted to see what had happened, others to complain about the noise waking them near midnight. Tez used his key to stop the noise, apologised pointlessly for the disturbance, and turned down the offer to call the police. As the crowd broke up he looked inside the garage. It was empty, just as he had left it. His gamble had paid off. Someone had come for his car. Luckily he had moved it somewhere more secret. Leaving the door open Tez went back to bed, checking the app on his phone to make sure the car hadn't moved. Slowly he slipped into an unsettled sleep.

Tuesday rolled along eventually and Tez felt the strange urge to domesticate himself. Almost a nesting desire it seemed to him that he should be able to cook, clean and care for his new lady, and treat her as such. The nagging fear still lurked at the back of his mind like a stalking lioness, but the hormones and primal urges of the male human being are strong and difficult to ignore. After another normal and uneventful day at work Tez stopped off by his flat only to park his bike, grab a big rucksack and check the cupboards. Armed with an actual shopping list he walked the mile to the supermarket situated on the edge of the shopping centre. It was a five mile drive around the town's mad one way system, and the narrow clogged streets made it feel longer. Through the back alleys and over parks Tez made it to the big blue signed supermarket within twenty minutes, a mild sweat forming on his brow. He checked his phone, irritated it had taken him so long. He used to do a mile in half the time. He was getting slow. Making a mental note to up his exercise Tez unrolled his crumpled list and roamed the aisles hoping to stumble over the things he needed.

An hour later, hoping the advice from the pretty girl stacking fruit was right, Tez paid, and filled his pack. In went fresh potatoes, carrots, peas in shells, Brussels sprouts, herbs, fresh seasoning, olive oil, flour, eggs, chocolate and a long line of other things for his grand idea. As he left the shop, shaking the pack to fit more comfortably on his shoulders, he checked his phone again, and headed home.

Pleased he had nearly reached his preferred time, albeit dripping in sweat and breathless, Tez laid out his shopping on the tiny worktop in his tiny kitchen. Sorting it into starter, main and dessert he checked the recipes and searched the cupboards for the right bowls and pans to cook it. On the counter his phone danced around, telling him he had a text message. With still sweaty hands Tez read the message from Christine. 'Would love to come tonight for tea, but busy. Can do tomorrow? Love C'. With a sigh of sorrow mixed with relief Tez packed everything into the fridge, ignoring the labels on how to store it all, and headed for the shower.

Wednesday night went on holiday for a while, making Tez wait for what seemed a month before it finally caught up with him. As soon as he got home at half 6 Tez went into action. Wishing he had practised he chopped, peeled, boiled and drained his vegetables, finally making a half decent stew. He never asked if she was a vegetarian so he kept meat out of it. For starter he made a passable melon hedgehog complete with raisin eyes and a cherry nose, and dessert was chocolate cake, a bit damp but very edible. The frozen half baked bread was nearly finished when there came a soft knock from the door. Cursing himself for not making time to shower Tez wiped his hands as best he could and opened the door.

First thing Christine noticed was the steam. She could

hardly see Tez through the sauna like cloud. The next thing was the heat. Finally came the smell of fresh baked bread, chocolate and home cooking. Her stomach rolled in glee at the thought of good home made food. She always cooked for her dad and usually it was what she could make from the dregs of the fridge. This smelt organised, prepared.

First thing Tez noticed was the very low cut short top she wore, making her appear like a Roman bust statue on a designed plinth. Her cleavage heaved sensually, making Tez feel weak. She had a new piercing hanging from her belly, a motorbike he noticed. He stood back to let her in, trying to look above her chest, and she shuffled in, her tight skirt and killer heels making walking a challenge.

As Tez excused himself and darted back into the kitchen Christine was left alone in the steam. As with most women when they first see their man's home she roamed the room with her eyes, taking it all in. The bed was a nice double, with smart cotton sheets. Had he had silk she would have worried. The TV wasn't a massive atrocity, but a fairly small affair, not dwarfing the room. There was a book case filled with a few tatty novels, some owner's manuals for cars and bikes, and some racing journals. On the wall hung pictures. Hundreds of them. With feminine curiosity Christine went from picture to picture, amazed. Here was Tez, a lot younger, with an older man and woman, parents maybe? All were posing by a clean family car. There was an older Tez on a dirt bike, covered in mud, his smile pure white in the brown. Another of Tez in racing overalls by an open car door, arm resting on the roof. Logos and sponsors stickers covered the outside, and the interior was stripped clean, only a seat and roll cage left. One caught her eye the most. It was small but placed prominently in the middle of the larger frames. It was a professional image from a studio. Tez, a little younger than the man in the kitchen, sat on an arm chair, smiling. On his lap with the same goofy smile was a girl a few years younger. With one hand on the chair's wing back, the other on his sons shoulder stood dad. Arm around her husband stood mum. It all seemed so fake, yet also so real. The smiles, the hands, the postures. Nobody ever sat like that as a family, but there was something in there.

"Old one, that," Tez said, making her jump. They both laughed, Christine just nodding her thanks when Tez gave her a cup of tea. She followed him into the kitchen, a tiny cheap build circa 1990 it had horrid white chipboard cabinets, a single oven mounted beside the grey worktop that stretched around two sides of the room in an L shape. The door in from the bedroom, and the one out to the bathroom, were half way down the other two walls, standing watch over the small wood table was only one chair.

Christine took the offered chair, Tez disappearing to find another. The steam had gradually cleared, a small window letting it out into the warm night. She felt sweat trickle down her back, and hoped her top didn't show any damp patches. Tez came back with a folding camping chair that left him sitting with the table at eye level. Christine laughed even more at the sight of Tez peeping over the table top at her like a puppy, and she felt her heart skip a beat. She shivered even in the heat.

Tez stood with some effort and served his melon, with a flamboyant and terrible French accent.

"Madame? Le melon, for you," he said, swooping the plate down and nearly firing the melon hedgehog into the wall. A quick flick saved it, although it lost an eye.

"Merci, Monsieur Tez," she giggled, and ate the spikes

from the hedgehog. Tez ate his, but his low position meant he stared at his starter face to cherry nosed face. Once both hedgehogs were shaved Tez swooped the plates away, managing by pure luck, to unintentionally fling them into the open bin. Christine applauded, then stood as Tez bowed almost to his knees, one arm out behind him, the other over his belly. He took the chance to look her up and down as he bowed. Once re-seated, and calm, Christine was served a bowl of vegetable stew, announcing she did eat meat, but the thought he had given was touching. Tez didn't taste the food, his senses were all used just on the image of the young woman opposite. Stew finished, Tez burnt himself on the pan, then took the chocolate cake out of a cupboard, and with two small plates and a knife he cut two generous slices, placing one before her.

"I may struggle with this," Christine said, eyeing the cake.

Fear stole over Tez's face. "You don't like chocolate?" he asked.

"I love it, what girl doesn't? Give me a cake and a bottle of wine and I'm in for the night," she laughed. "But after all this I don't know if I have the space. Gotta keep my figure, you know?"

Tez, who had been admiring the figure all night just nodded, absently stabbing his slice with a spoon. Christine fell silent, and they looked at each other over the cake.

There wasn't a spark, or a twinkle, not even signal from the eyes, but like two opposite magnets they drew closer slowly, until when they were almost nose to nose they closed their eyes, tilted their heads to their right, and kissed.

Later that night Christine lay in his bed and fought her

feelings. Part of her was happy they had finally slept together. Between her legs still tingled, the feeling of him inside her made her want it again. He felt so perfect. Just the right size, and he knew how to use it. Her clothes lay on the floor, mixed with his, where they had been dropped in the short passionate three legged walk from the table to the bed. Another part, the logical part in her head, felt relief she had met a man who cared as much as he did, looked as good as he did. He was so gentle, until she screamed for him to really use her, which he did. And man did it feel good. Another part felt fear, of a new relationship, and the unknown. True she looked a bit cheap, dressing like she charges by the hour, but that was to get the customers in, to roll up the tips, to make the night pass. She had been with another man before, but after a drunken night, and she didn't see him again. This felt different, scary, but exciting.

Tez slept with one arm under her neck, one leg over her belly. His face, so serene and peaceful was close enough to kiss again. She saw her lipstick smeared on his face, tracing a fading red trail to his ear, then down his neck. That face seemed innocent, unknowing of the truth she hid. That truth made her feel dirty, like a real hooker, giving herself for cash, earning off the carnal desires of men. With his sweat drying on her chest, his soft breathing in her ear, Christine tried very hard not to cry.

10

Sunlight struggled to break through the Thursday

morning cloud, casting irregular shadows on the scattered clothes. Tez's alarm rang, shrill and annoying. Groaning he opened his eyes, right into Christine's. Peace, almost joy, spread over his face, hers mirroring him. Then shock, fear and surprise hit both simultaneously. They both sat upright, ignoring their nakedness and started talking frantically.

"Oh, shit. I'm gonna be late," cried Tez, while Christine just repeated; "Dad's gonna kill me" over and over. They pulled underwear, socks and everything else on in a rush, Christine stifling a giggle when Tez put his work shirt on backwards. He swore again, turned it around, giving her a last glimpse of his toned chest. She pulled her top over her breasts, trying to poke them into place, and wiggled into her skirt. Wobbling on high heels she headed for the door.

"That, that was great. Thank you," she said, pausing by the door, hand on the snick lock.

Tez looked up from the bed as he sat doing his laces up. "Yeah, it was. Gotta do it again."

"Tonight?" Christine was shocked to hear her own words, so keen.

Tez seemed surprised too, but he smiled. "Yeah, you know where I live."

She laughed, erasing the worry on her smooth face, lingered a moment longer to take in his face, and fled into the chilly morning. Tez sat a while, thinking. The room was cold from the window that he left open all night, but it still smelled of sex, passionate and frantic. He stretched, pissed in the lavatory, and grabbed his jacket.

He arrived at work just in time. Hurriedly opening the roller doors, and nearly setting off the alarm, he push his bike inside, made a cup of tea and wiped the sweat from his unshaven face as the first of the mechanics turned up, not noticing the change in him. He was happier, more relaxed, even cheerful. When he joined in with the banter they were suspicious, then surprised, and finally they let him join in, a little relieved he seemed normal. Hopdyke noticed too, hooded eyes watching from the other side of the yard, no joy, just worry and fear on his face. After a long internal deliberation he went and called his company insurance, just to check, and raise the estimated value. You can't be too careful.

In the Bull Christie sneaked in through the front door, instead of the side door they usually used. She knew her dad would have been up all night, and if he was asleep in the kitchen she could get past him, upstairs, then come down as if she had been home all night. It didn't work. Face down on a table like a drunk her dad snored loudly, empty pint glass in one hand. She passed him on tiptoes, but as she came near him his free hand shot out and grabbed her arm.

"Where the hell have you been?" he asked.

Christie stood, waiting for the lecture. He was in one of his bad moods. They were more common now.

"I asked you a question." His head was still on the table, other hand on the glass.

"Out."

"Out," he repeated. Alvin slowly raised his head. Christie choked back a laugh at the beer mat stuck to his cheek. His expression behind the mat helped her. "Do you think I'm stupid?"

"Dad," she began but his grip on her arm tightened briefly.

"You listen to me, girl, and you listen good. Sit."

She sat. facing him over the table she reached over and gently pulled the mat from his face. He gave a brief thankful look, then hardened.

"I know it's been hard, without your mum and all, but I gotta take care of you. I ain't no decent dad, not a bloke who deserves a daughter like you. I screw up, a lot."

"Dad," she started again but he held up a hand.

"Don't. Hear me out." Alvin paused, eyes searching hers.

After eternity he spoke. "You been out whoring?"

Christie almost slapped him, before realising it was her father, who loved her, and meant it as a question, not an insult.

"No, Dad. How the hell can you ask that? Why?"

Alvin shook his head. "Because Colin Hopwood came over late last night. Gave me back some of the IOU's from our poker games. Said you had helped repay them. He paying you for it?"

Christie felt her face burn, tears began to well. "No, Dad. I never went with him. I never would."

"Look at me, girl. I want no secrets and lies between us. It's us against the world. Can't be us against us."

"No lies? Dad. How deep are you in debt? Honest."

"Enough to keep me up at night."

"Dad." The word was a threat. Alvin saw his lost love in his daughter's face, in her voice, and shuddered.

"He could claim half the pub," he said, unable to resist.

"Dad! How could you lose half the Bull?" Christie was shocked to near speechlessness. She knew it was a lot, she had been told by Colin, but not that much.

"I ain't lost it."

"You said."

Alvin glared at her. "I said he could claim it. He ain't. He gets free beer, cheap booze and parties for his gang, and I get to play his poker buddies twice a month."

"And lose more money? Dad you gotta stop, and stop now."

"And how do I pay him off? If I don't play he'll just claim it, all legal like. I don't lose often. The doctor comes out worse normally."

Christie pulled her hand free and rubbed the tears from her eyes. "So what we gonna do, Dad?"

"We do nothing, but find out what you been doing to pay it off, if not lying on your back."

She looked away for a moment, but he saw it.

"You did lay someone last night, didn't you?" He stared at her bowed head, into the dark roots of her blonde hair. Her shoulders sagged, tears dropping slowly on the varnished table top. She said nothing.

Resisting the urge to hold her in his arms Alvin leant back instead. "I ain't got no say in your life, and if you did it to help me, I thank you. But I don't want you out whoring any more. I'd rather we lost the pub, then you lose your dignity."

"I wasn't whoring," she said, head still down.

"What then?"

"Dad, I met someone." She looked up, eyes red. "He's a decent guy, with a decent job, and has his own flat."

Relief washed Alvin's face free of most of the lines of age. "Really? Why the hell didn't you say, you silly bitch." He had his big dopey grin on, the one she had nearly forgotten it had been so long in coming.

"Really, Dad. He works for Hopdyke's in town. Comes from Derby way. He can cook, talk a load of languages, and he's fit as hell."

Alvin grimaced. "Didn't need that last bit. So you stayed at his then?"

She nodded. "Yeah. He made me the most romantic meal."

"Good for you. I had cheese on toast when I closed the bar, which I ran alone all night."

"Sorry, Dad."

Alvin waived a hand vaguely. "No bother. How did you meet?"

Christie opened her mouth to speak, but the truth stuck to her tongue. Instead the smiled and stood. "I need my beauty sleep, and you really need it, so why don't we go to bed for a bit, then later I can tell all?"

Yawning Alvin nodded, stood, and let his little girl push him to the stairs.

Thursday was the best day at work Tez had had for years. The guys all accepted him straight away, making him the butt of most of the day's jokes, but he enjoyed it as much as they did. They were all almost sad when 6 came along and they had to go. They all pitched in to lock up, and with some last jokes and insults they went their separate ways. Tez was still smiling as he headed out the yard, and towards the point where he met Christine. The smile was taken from him like a cherished toy from a child by the blue lights in his small mirrors. Slowing down the lights pulled in behind. Cursing his luck Tez thumbed a right indicator and pulled over.

Sergeant Henry Forbes had been on the beat since he was old enough to join. He lived in town, and always would. From birth all he knew was Lower Hampton and that was all he cared about. He knew most of the trouble makers, their folks, and friends. This new kid he didn't, but he was going to now. He lifted his slightly overweight frame from one of the three Vauxhall Insignia's the station had, put on his best highway patrol swagger, and waited for the punk on the bike to take off his helmet.

"You know why I stopped you?" he asked.

Tez had done this many times before, so kept his face friendly, his voice neutral. "No, Sergeant. Was I speeding?"

"No, you weren't speeding, kid. This your bike?"

Tez nodded. "All up to date and safe."

"Good." Forbes waddled around the bike, as if searching for faults. Finally he looked up. "You Terrence Belkin?"

"Yeah, why?"

Forbes smiled. "Need to take you in. For questioning."

Tez opened his mouth to complain, then snapped it shut. Forbes didn't take out the handcuffs, but he did open the back door to his car. Sat on the semi comfortable seats Tez was more than a little annoyed. He hadn't even done anything wrong. Instinctively he tested the door handle to see if the child locks were on. They were. Trapped in the car he waited while the fat copper chatted on the radio strapped to his shoulder. After ten minutes one of the other marked cars came, with an extra man to ride the bike to the station. Forbes got in, and without saying a word turned the car around drove them to the old police station.

Parking in the small yard out back next to the third patrol car Tez was let out of the back and, still uncuffed, he was led past the duty sergeant and into one of the questioning rooms. Alone he tried to think of why he was there. Time dragged, an old police trick of making the suspect sweat. Tez had been there too often to let that happen. He leant back, rested his feet on the table, yawned and tried to sleep. The door rattled open, jerking him back. In sauntered Henderson, a thick blue foolscap folder in his hand. He sat down opposite, and with one hand on the other over the folder he simply stared at Tez. Tez stared back. The first battle of will had begun. Tez had no idea why he was there, but feared his past had caught him. If Henderson knew his past there was nothing Tez could do to get away, so just say nothing.

Henderson saw the punk kid knew what was going on, had been there before. The folder held Tez's entire criminal history, and those of his previous associates. There was a lot to read. Henderson never gave in to the will war against any opponent, but he knew time was pressing. Without charges the kid could walk in hours, and in this day and age he could sue them for time wasting, some pansy lawyer getting him a nice big cheque and a picture in the local rag. Bad for the police, worse for Henderson's career. Although he never lost a battle, he never lost the war either. This was a skirmish, one he could lose, or let slide, in order to get the main prize.

To say Inspector Marvin Henderson disliked crime was the same as saying the Atlantic Ocean was a big lake. From his youth he first disliked, then loathed, and finally hated with a passion those who stepped outside the boundaries of normal, decent people. He saw himself as the guardian of peace, a gun slinger on the new frontier, a frontier of gang mobs, thieves and crooks all fighting each other, which suited Henderson, and the law, which didn't. Five year's ago that little inter-family spat had led to the deaths of five hoodlum yobs, injury to four others, and two innocent members of the public being hurt enough to warrant hospital treatment. The expense of dealing with the massive riot style fist fight was enough to pale any prisoner rights' activist. To the town it was a blot on the frayed tapestry of it's history, to Henderson it was a personal slur on his name. He hadn't gotten a single conviction. Everyone had an alibi, or were not involved, or just not there. Both the Hopwood kids had vanished early on once knives were drawn. After the warning tape had been pulled down, blood stained sawdust swept up, closed roads opened, these two young men had the best alibi. They were out of town on a family holiday. The fact they hated each other, the fight had been about them, that they had thrown the first punches was immaterial. Their stupid parents had vouched for them in court, more points to them, more egg on Henderson's face. With reviews looming on his position, and promotions walking out in the hands of lesser officers he had no choice but to seal the deal, cuff and stuff them, name your conditions. All he cared about was having them both in these rooms, charged and squealing confessions so he could ditch this crappy town and head to the big cities, where crime and promotions lay in wait for him to ensnare.

Tez tried not to smile at the stupidity of his situation. Here he was either waiting for an apology for holding him, or the axe to fall if his past was found out. He knew he'd done wrong, and he'd been ridiculously lucky. When the house he'd shared was raided for drugs, guns and money he'd been out, or the house had been empty. His friends got the convictions, Tez got slaps on his wrist. They didn't hate him for that. They knew he was lucky, always had been. It was the luck of the draw, and Tez played his cards well. That made it worse. Had they blamed him he could have accepted it. It was their dumb faith in him to lead them to better things, the high life. He led them instead to a prison cell. Some leader. Now he was either gonna join them, or walk out. All in all a pretty stupid place to be.

Henderson made a pretence of reading the file, even though both knew he would have memorised it all. The stuffy room was thick with tension, so strong it made the hairs on your neck stand up. Tez knew he could wait, his bike would wait, but he did worry. He worried about Christine, what she was doing. Was she trying to call him?

Hopdyke wouldn't care about this, same as his grumpy land lord, who only cared the flat was clean and the rent paid on time. Henderson tried to look nonchalant, but the tension poured into him like water into a hole in a ships hull. He knew he was sinking, and he needed to bail out. Maybe try to turn the kid? Use him? Send him undercover? Inside he dismissed the idea. How could he trust some petty thug with his own future? Best to make sure he stayed out of it.

Leaning forwards Henderson closed the file and leant on it, hands clasped almost as if he were praying. Tez, sensing the start of the interview proper, took a breath and locked eyes on the copper.

"Terrence Belkin, 29, lives flat 4A, Grove Mews." Henderson didn't say it as a question, and Tez kept silent. "You know why you are here, boy." Tez shook his head.

"You know what's happening in this town?" Henderson asked.

"Nope," Tez replied, shaking his head briefly.

Henderson sighed. "You know. I know you know. Only an old granny with more teeth then brain cells could miss the gangs. I know about your history, Belkin. I know what you did, and where. I know you raced, hell, you could have gone pro. But you didn't. Instead you wasted it, and let your buddies take the rap for it. I don't care about that. I care about cleaning the crap out of here. I'm like a plumber, they call for me, I come, clear the drains, then go. I know you ain't doing anything stupid. Your car's been seen out and about, but only at night, hidden. Keep it that way. I don't want to ever see you, or your car, in my mirrors, or hear your plate or name on my radio. Understand?"

Tez, who was completely lost, just nodded. He felt like a bankrupt finding a winning lottery ticket.

Henderson stood, keeping eye contact, trying to force his point more, and left. Tez let out his breath and rubbed his face. Another copper came in and led him to the yard where his bike was. On autopilot Tez pulled his helmet on and left.

The police canteen was upstairs at the back of the station overlooking the yard. Ignoring the few off duty police officers there Henderson went straight to the dirty window and watched the kid leave. He was aware everyone was looking at him, Bicks included. He knew the kid was the key, the 'get out of jail free' card. Henderson would bring the whole house of cards down on him, one way or another.

This was his chance, and he was going to use it.

11

That evening the sun drooped in a lazy heat haze, bathing the valley in orange glow, bouncing off the walls in crazy shadows. Mark Hopwood was testing the big Kawasaki's latest retune on the hills, letting the bike do the work, taking corners and bumps in a relaxed, easy flow. He knew the roads well enough to push hard, but he never felt pushed. His old bike, a great long big sports tourer, used to fly on the straights, but was a bit of a handful on the bends. This new bike, only out a few years, was still a cruise missile, but turned like it was on rails, and was as easy to ride as a push bike, just no peddling. Inside, in the back of his mind, Mark knew he was going to win this year. Finally he could lay the stupid feud to rest. He wasn't vindictive, he had no interest in evicting his own blood. Both could stay, but as one group, cars and bikes. No more fighting, no more silly wars, no more grief.

As the bike ate up the road Mark saw the new kid's car pull into the overlook car park. He did think a lot on that car. It wasn't subtle, sponsor stickers and a body wrap job making it look every inch the race car. He had heard it was fast, but if the kid joined Colin's group he would be racing it, not Colin. It could be a threat, but a minor one. Even in his rage Colin wouldn't steal a car just to win, or have anyone hurt. Throwing the thought away to the road Mark twisted the throttle a little more and went for the next corner.

Tez had managed to get home before Christine messaged him. With the long summer nights still bright her suggestion of a picnic tea sounded perfect. He picked her up from near her house, she still never showed him where she really lived, and drove to the overlook car park, wicker basket sliding around in the stripped out boot. Reverse parking so the car faced the entrance Tez took the hamper, and blanket Christine had brought, and walked past the benches, choosing a nice spot half in the sun, half in the shade of an old tree. Christine loved sitting in the sun, Tez didn't, so he laid out the check blanket with the shadow covering half, and opened the hamper.

Inside were plastic tubs of cold chicken legs, pies, sausages, cakes and snacks. A large bottle of fizzy pop and two plastic cups were tucked down the side. Letting Christine lie in the sun, the light making her tanned belly glow, Tez took the lids off the tubs, and arranged them as best he could. They ate in silence, lost in the aura of the town laid below like a model village. When there was nothing but crumbs and bones in the tubs Christine dropped them back into the hamper. The sun had moved, leaving them completely in it's beam. Tez lay back, Christine beside, one arm on his stomach, one leg over his. He felt it grow firm under that leg, sure she must feel it too, or at least see it through his jeans. Her head rested on his chest, hair tickling his cheek. Holding her like this Tez suddenly felt old, mature. It was as if adulthood had finally arrived, bringing responsibilities and dull monotony of old age. He knew he was in love, the girl who was now snoring gently on his chest had finally taken his heart. He couldn't leave any more than he could cut off his own hand. He still felt unease, something not quite right.

  Craning his head to check on his car he could only see the rear spoiler over the rise of the hill. The movement woke Christine, who mumbled something and fell silent again. Looking around at the blanket, the hamper, the girl, Tez had an image of his parents doing this, maybe years before them. The date, the romantic walks, the closeness. Ok, none of his family would be with a girl who wore denim miniskirts and high heels to a picnic, and none would wear make up or fake tan, but he wasn't his dad, or granddad. He was who he was.

  A slow realisation dawned, like first man realising if the stone is round it moves easier. He was him. Nobody else. He can make his own way, do his own thing. Why worry about the past? It's the past. Look to the past for education, the future for inspiration. Tez would carve his own future, thank you very much. He was going to do it his way, and stuff that copper, the gangs, the rules. Life was for living, and he was going to live it. Christine was snoring again. Tez smiled at the warm sun and closed his eyes, seeing the red glow through his eyelids. He was going to do his own thing, when he woke up. Still grinning he dozed off, still holding the girl. He didn't hear the bike pull up in the car park, idle for a minute or so, then leave.

Tez was beginning to feel more than a little uncomfortable taking the car out, knowing both the gangs, the law and the neighbours were on the look out for it. To be safe he moved it again, using a lock up that he persuaded Hopdyke to rent in his name. This left him with the bike alone, not ideal for dates. He did consider asking Christine to move in, but he knew it was too early. He didn't want the love to burn up too fast, but keep the flames fanned and hot. Thinking on alternatives he could have found another car, one he could tune to his tastes. That seemed wrong, selfish even. Christine was still roaming in a crap old car that smoked, clunked and looked the opposite to the young lady driving it. One Saturday evening he texted her, asking her over to see a film. Claiming his car was off the road he asked her to drive them. As usual she came five minutes late, trying to do something with her hair while she drove.

"You look ace, as usual," Tez said, getting in before she could say anything. "Drive on."

She gave him a look that would curdle milk still in the cow and struggled with the gear stick, the box grinding painfully. Finally they kangarooed out onto the road, Tez hiding a laugh badly.

When they got to cinema in the west end shopping area the old Corsa wheezed and clunked into space, letting out a sigh and a small puff of blue smoke. Tez waited outside while Christine manually locked his door. As they walked to the cinema Tez hooked his arm around her waist, feeling the clammy skin of her back. He pulled her gently closer to him, her left arm around his waist, hand in his back jeans pocket. Halfway there Tez stopped and wheeled them both around to face the car.

"What?" she asked, thinking he'd forgotten something.

Tez paused, eyeing the old red Vauxhall. Finally he said, "you know, with a bit of effort, that could be a serious bit of kit."

Christine first looked puzzled, then irritated. Tez smiled.

"Babe, you shouldn't be driving a pile of crap, it really isn't you. Give me the car for the week, and let me make it a bit more," he kissed her gently, "you," he finished.

Her green eyes flitted back and forth searching her man's, searching for lies, false promises, deceit. There was none. Holding back the tears she smiled, absently playing with the stud in her nose.

"You'd do that? Why?" she asked.

Tez pulled away, walking a few steps and turning to face her.

"I see you there, nice clothes, hell of a body, a face that could launch a thousand ships, and a heart of pure perfection." Reaching out Tez opened his arms like a parent to a toddler learning to walk. Christine felt drawn into his embrace. He held her tight, almost painful. "You are the best bloody thing to happen to me in my whole crappy life. If you are staying with me we need you rolling with style."

Christine didn't try to move, but spoke into his chest. "Why though? I never did anything for you. All the money you'll need to make that look half decent. It's not worth it."

"It's yours," replied Tez into the top of her head. "That makes it priceless. Old Corsa's are easy to mod anyway. You may be surprised how cheap it can be. Need my baby safe and stylish."

Christine realised the relationship had taken a leap. He'd never called her 'babe' or any pet name before. His embrace, still strong, almost felt desperate, as if he clung to her for his own safety more then hers. Something clicked inside and she felt strangely self conscious. Inside the little voice that rarely spoke now screamed at her. It screamed about the debts, her deal, the car not even really hers. Guilt, anger, shame, sorrow and pain all whirled around like an icy wind in her veins. She gripped his t shirt in clenched fists, burying her head into his firm chest, biting back the feeling of utter wretchedness. She was dressed like a hooker, being paid, no, blackmailed like a hooker, and the worst part was the guy she was playing didn't know. And she didn't want to do it any more. She didn't want the pain he would feel when the truth came out.

Tears flowing freely she pushed him away and ran on tottering heels to the car. He stood, lost, and watched her scrabble with the keys, open the car and drive away. Feeling numb Tez watched the brake lights flash at the entrance to the centre, and the car vanished into the street. A warm, late summer breeze tugged gently at his creased shirt, but he felt a shiver. Still mystified the logical part of his brain took over and gently guided him home.

Monday morning when Tez rode into work, the red car was there, an envelope under one wiper blade. Leaving his bike in the middle of the yard Tez opened it in gloved hands, flipping his visor open. Inside was a hand written note on purple paper, and the keys.

'Tez. Sorry for Saturday. We need to talk and some is good, some is bad. Do the car, if you like, but I understand if you don't wanna. I'll meet you next weekend, back at La Fam, Sat, at half seven. Please forgive me. Love Christie.'

Holding the note, almost smiling at the little hearts on the 'i's Tez felt more lost than ever. He knew something strange, almost restricted. She loved him, he knew that, felt that. But something was stopping her fully committing. Maybe in part that was why he didn't ask her to move in. It never felt the right time. A million reasons flashed through his mind. She had another man, she was pregnant, she was married, she had a sexual illness, she had a terminal illness, her family were crazy.

Tez was a rare person. When faced with hurdles in life he didn't panic, or worry, or go over the top. Instead he'd stop, think, then act. Opening up the garage he passively joined in with the banter. The cars were repaired properly, methodically. All the jobs were done on time. Outside Tez seemed engrossed in his work. Inside his mind raced like an engine. Considering options and scenarios. How to deal with this, how to react to that. At home time he said his goodbyes, locked up and rode home. Tuesday the paint shop was quiet, so without asking permission Tez rolled the Corsa in. After a quick chat to the girls in the parts shop his orders were made and Tez began stripping the car. Feeling like an extra on Pimp My Ride he worked hard, sourcing parts from breakers, other garages, even on line. By Saturday afternoon the transformation was complete and, having left the bike at home, Tez rolled out the garage to congratulations from his co-workers, and an irritated nod of appreciation from Hopdyke. Leaving the guys to lock up Tez headed for the hills.

While her car raced the country lanes Christie tried to work out what she was going to do. Inside she felt torn, as if one half was tied to a tree, the other to a car. She wanted to call off the deal, but if she did then her dad would lose the pub. If she didn't though, she would lose her soul. The dilemma went far beyond any soap on TV. Her dad knew something was up from the previous Saturday when she ran in crying, past a half full bar of regulars, and upstairs. The slamming of her bedroom door, childlike, said well enough she wanted to be alone. Making light of it Alvin joked as he pulled pints, eyes unsmiling, focused on the bar end door. That night he went to bed when the bar was closed, and passing her door the soft sounds of crying still came through the thick wood. More then ever wishing her mum was still there Alvin dropped his head and went to bed.

The next day was as if nothing had happened. Her cheery voice, singing of all things, had woken him from a troubled sleep. Downstairs the bar gleamed. The taps were polished, the dark stained bar top cleaned and the bar mats spinning in the wash. The floor was swept and mopped, tables cleaned, windows washed and the toilets sluiced out. Christie was singing loudly with a massive smile, her soft voice carrying well the tune in her head. Many had said she was good on the karaoke, some suggested going professional. Now she nearly danced around the kitchen, bacon frying on the old hob, freshly devoid of the years of grease that had built up. Toast browned in the toaster while the kettle clicked off. On the old wooden table lay the morning papers, a plate awaiting the scrambled eggs, bacon and toast, and a large mug with a tea bag in.

Christie had motioned him to sit.

"You ok?" Alvin had asked.

"Sure, Dad," she'd replied, kissing his unshaven cheek before dancing out the kitchen to see the delivery man who'd just arrived. Confused and disturbed Alvin collected the various breakfasts cooking and ate.

Now it was a week later and he still worried. He had thought this new man was doing something, making her do things she shouldn't. Alvin knew a cover when he saw it, and she was covering something big. Her car had gone, but Colin kept coming up, speaking to her instead of him. Alvin knew she knew about the debt, but was the younger Hopwood boy involved?

The bar was slowly filling up even though it was only half six. Christie had vanished hours ago, the old boiler clunking into life so she must be having a bath. Wondering if she was going to help tonight he considered popping upstairs, but decided against it. She'd been strange all week, last thing he needed was her going crazy on a Saturday. She would talk when she was ready. She always did.

The bar end door opened and Christie strode past with all the purpose of a business woman going to the most important meeting of her career. Dressed in a knee length skirt, a top that reached her belt and sensible shoes she still wore make up, but more subtly. She waved a hand in farewell, passed the silenced bar, and left.

"'ere, Alvin?" asked an old regular, staring at the door she'd just left through.

"Yeah, Freddy?" said Alvin, looking the same way.

"Was that your young 'un?"

"Maybe, maybe not."

"Ah," said Freddy, turning back to his pint of beer. Alvin kept looking at the door for a moment, then shook his head. He had customers to serve.

Christie had booked the taxi two days before. In her head she hoped she'd finally decided what to do. Dressed in her mum's more sensible clothes, she was going to be an adult. 'Tell all and shame the devil' her mum used to say. She'd written a note to Colin, saying she needed to see him, but left it in her room. Tez was what concerned her more. She expected a fight, maybe even a curse shouting, chair throwing row. If he never wanted to see her again she would understand. But it would be over, and it would be out.

No more hiding, no more secrets eating away at her.

In the back of the taxi she watched the town pass by. Nerves, fear and anticipation made her jumpy, playing absently with her painted nails, no more false ones now. Tez would meet the mature, adult Christine, not the childish Christie, the woman, not the slut, the adult not the child.

She got to the La Famiglia ten minutes early so she got herself a red wine, considered for a moment, then downed half the glass. The staff noticed her, and some remembered her. The other diners noticed an attractive young lady in a stylish dress, nice shoes and a pretty face. At half seven Christine sat at the tiny bar near the entrance. She heard a loud exhaust warble in, rev a bit as the driver parked, then silence. Finishing the wine she took a deep breath. The door opened and Tez came in, dressed in his usual jeans, but a nice pale blue shirt on top that showed his muscles nicely. She felt a rise of passion, of sexual arousal, and pushed it down. He hadn't come over, just stood in the doorway looking stupid. Finally she realised he didn't recognise her. With a grin she waved to him, noticing the realisation dawn on his handsome face.

"Wow," he said, eyeing up the dress.

"You like?" she asked, slipping off the bar stool and giving a twirl.

"Kinda, yeah."

She stopped. "Kinda?"

Panic crossed his face. "I mean, yeah, just, it's a lot different."

"Good," she said playfully, and led him to a corner of the restaurant so they had some privacy. Speaking slowly she explained her dad's debt, the deal she had made with Colin, the situation with her car and how she really loved

Tez. By the end she was crying quietly, eyes red and pleading. He hadn't moved. Waiting in silence she searched his blank face for a sign, anything. Without moving his eyes Tez stood and left. Feeling even worse Christine dropped her head into her hands, shoulders rocking. A hand rested gently on her arm. With running make up she saw through the blur of tears Tez looking down at her. His half smile was back.

"You stupid, dozy cow," he said. Dropping her car keys onto the table he smiled and left.

12

Tez walked home following the roads. He didn't want to be seen by anyone, but how he felt at the moment the chances were he'd get lost going cross country. Though the tears fell they were slow, like gentle rain. His mind swam, making him feel drunk. The enormity of what had happened swamped like waves. He knew there was something, but not that big. How could anyone live like that? How could a human treat someone that way?

Anger, shock, pain and sorrow mingled with helplessness and shame, brewing a cocktail of base emotions. His initial reaction was to walk, to leave. What stopped him leaving were the feelings he held for Christine, his love, the solid ache in his heart. Like a lead weight she held him down, stopped him floating. He couldn't leave her any more then he could cut off his fingers. But he had to help her. This was something that had to end.

As he walked Tez calmed. The road ahead lay as clear as day, both the tarmac street, and the path he had to take to solve the issues. Unknowingly, Christine had told him all he needed to know. How much her dad owed, what was happening beneath the surface, the random visits by Henderson, and the Hopwood men. Slowly, like a detective story, it unravelled as he walked. By the time the 'Welcome to Lower Hampton' sign came into view Tez was jogging comfortably. He used to do distance running in school and still could get the miles in. Taking the back streets to his flat he kept looking out for her car. Reaching home undisturbed he pulled a large case from the back of the wardrobe. With a smile of satisfaction he unzipped it.

In La Famiglia Christine accepted the fifth tissue from the cute barman, smiled weakly and thanked him. They were out the back of the restaurant, away from the public. Her first thought was to chase after Tez, try to explain better, but she knew that would only make it worse. He needed time, and space. She then thought of her car, but the staff asked her politely to head out the back, away from the customers, away from eyes. With another glass of wine, on the house, she relaxed enough to see the barman was trying to hit on her, and felt flattered. In her mum's nice clothes she felt strange, older and more mature. Not herself. Worried the wine would make her go over the drive limit she pushed it away, thanked the man, giving him a fake phone number, and left.

The car outside was as far from the battered old wreck Colin had given her as you could imagine. Instead of flaky red paint, dented panels and a chipped windscreen there sat a smooth, rich, pink hatchback, lowered to the floor on race suspension. Repaired wheel arches sat over dark grey alloy wheels, an expensive make too. The glass was all new, tinted a dark shade of pink to match the bodywork. Inside the seats were re-trimmed in dark leather with pink piping. The gauges and clocks were all new, white with pink accent lights, and a flip out touch screen radio replaced the old tape deck. Settling into the semi bucket drivers seat she took a deep breath and keyed the ignition. The starter spun and fired, a deep bass rumble from the single oval pipe out the back. It didn't sound anything like the engine before. She saw a turbo boost gauge on the dash, unable to resist the urge to tap the gas pedal, watching the needle rise and fall. A sharp hiss from the dump valve almost made her jump. With over dramatic caution she selected first, and left the car park. Half looking out for her man Christine drove slowly until she came to a straight bit of road, then floored it. The car pinned her to the seat as it leapt forwards, tyres squealing. In panic she jammed on the brakes, nearly lifting the rear wheels as the massive front brakes gripped the discs. In the darkening road, engine idling, Christine tried to imagine the hours of work, and money spent, to make this car for her. Feeling her love explode inside she rested her head on the leather race steering wheel and tried not to cry again. A car behind honked in annoyance, so she gently drove off, rubbing her eyes.

Alvin pulled his hundredth pint of the evening and inwardly cursed his daughter. Saturdays were always busy, and this was no exception. The warm weather, late nights, and convenient location of the Black Bull meant it was packed. Unable to afford staff wages they ran it alone, and with her out chasing whatever Alvin had to hold the fort by himself. Glancing at the clock over the bar he was shocked it was already half past eight in the evening. Sunlight still speared through the frosted windows, highlighting the pub logo on the glass. The small bar was three deep in waiting drinkers, all holding wallets and purses ready. The humid evening air hardly reached the bar and Alvin had to use a bar towel to wipe the sweat from his balding face.

The sound of a loud exhaust made him flinch, and look out the open door. The 4power lot didn't meet this weekend, but only a few of them would cause chaos with the other punters, insisting they were served first, and to a table, as if they were in a posh cocktail bar. If Alvin was lucky one of their meets didn't end up with a broken window. He kept trying to meet the flow of requests, while keeping an eye on the door. He almost shouted in relief when Christie came in, wearing her mothers clothes. For a small and sad moment she looked the copy of her mum, tugging a long forgotten pain in his heart. Then the paternal instinct took over and he saw she had been crying. Unable to leave the bar he tried to wave to her, but she pushed past everyone, almost shouldered the bar end door off it's hinges and left. Torn between his desire to go to his child, and the responsibility of running the pub Alvin clenched his teeth, cursed the luck fairy for deserting him, and reached for another pint glass.

Upstairs Christine went to her room, dropped on the bed and cried into her pillow. Aware, and unashamed, she was acting the way she did as a small kid as she cried until the tears stopped, feeling the dull ache in her throat, soreness in her eyes, and shame on her cheeks. Sitting up on her bed, avoiding the damp patch, she bowed her head and thought. She wasn't a religious person, but she knew, somewhere, there was something, or someone, looking down over her. Her heart felt it, even if her head didn't believe. Now she spoke out inside, asking for help. She felt all the pain, excitement, shame and anger all over again. Fear gripped her. What if he never wanted to see her again? She didn't care if he told everyone, she deserved worse. But to live without him? Only now she realised how deeply she loved him, willing to lose her home, her family, even her self respect for this man she had been told to attract. From that morning when she had knocked him off his bike the warmth inside had started, growing, burning, until it took over her soul. Now that was gone, and the charred remains of her life smoked in the embers of loss.

Without knowing she fell asleep, exhausted from the turmoil brewing inside. Below her Alvin burned the ceiling with angry eyes, and served pint after sweaty pint until finally the crowds thinned, the glasses piled up, and the sun sank. Down to the last of almost everything he tidied as best he could between orders, collecting bottles and glasses, filling and emptying the glass washer, rearranging the tables. Night had settled fully now and only a few people remained, most unable to walk. The unofficial routine was for Alvin to nudge them to the back room, and let them sleep it off under the pool table. He was hoping it was the end of the night, one with minimal breakages and a lot of profit, when he heard the sound of a single motorbike stop outside. The only bikers were the Yoki lot, and they never met here. This was enemy territory. Alvin waited, glass basket in one hand watching the door. He felt no better when a man walked in.

The first thing Alvin noticed was the man looked the opposite of the usual drinker, in jeans and a biker jacket. He had no helmet, left on the bike, perhaps? In one hand he held a supermarket carrier bag, filled with what looked like small boxes. The other was in his pocket. The man looked straight at him.

"You Christine's dad?" the man asked.

Alvin put the basket down. "Yeah. Why?"

The man smiled. He was quite handsome, especially when he smiled. Alvin felt a shot of jealousy. This guy would never need a hot water bottle to warm his bed. The man sat at an empty table, put the bag by his feet, and motioned Alvin to sit opposite. Confused, he did so.

"Now then," started the man. "Apologies, but I never learnt your surname."

"Thorpe," said Alvin, eyes locked. The man didn't even blink.

"Mr Thorpe. I have something to tell you, about your daughter. Please bear with me, as it will be a shock, but she has done nothing wrong. In fact, she's done something amazing."

Alvin felt fear, anger and sadness all at once. He said nothing and after a moment the man spoke again, voice full of confidence and assured.

"Mr Thorpe, I have been the man, probably the only man, to have dated your daughter. She is an amazing young lady, someone who managed to break me from my past, and make me want to build a future. So I wanted to help her in return. You know the old car you gave her?"

"I didn't give her a car, she said it was a gift," Alvin said, dry mouthed.

"It was. You know a man called Colin Hopwood?" The man waited until Alvin had nodded. "I figured. He had you by the balls I think. Poker. Nasty game."

Alvin was now on the spiral corkscrew of the emotional roller coaster. Feeling numb, unable to speak let alone understand he sat in silence.

"I know he fiddled you out of cash, and a lot. Then he had power over you. Ever wondered why you lost so much at the start, then seemed to do ok after? He played you. I hate his kind of player. He had you by the ball sack, and knew how to squeeze. Then he turned on your daughter." The man paused, almost considering if to carry on. "He blackmailed her to his own ends. She was told to entice me, persuade me to join his little group, and give over something of mine so he could win a silly little bet. Dozy git may have won too, if she hadn't such a big heart. I think she loves me, I feel she does, but with all this crap going on I think she's scared too."

The man reached down and dropped the bag on the table. He stood, half turned, and hesitated.

"That's what you 'owe' that bastard. You can never be free with that chained to your life, and neither can Christine. I love her, and I want more than anything for her to be happy. You owe me nothing, she has done more than anyone could."

"You mean," began Alvin, fearing the worst.

"No, no," said the man. "Not like that. I never would, and she is too much of a lady. I came to this town a lost boy, now I leave a man. Not forever, but for a few days. Tell her I love her, and when I'm sorted I will come back to her."

The man walked to the door. Alvin stayed seated, but called out to him.

"Who loves her?" he asked.

The man stopped but didn't turn.

"Tell her," the man paused, looking at the emerging stars. "Tell her Tez will come back. That's a promise."

He left, the soft snores of the drunks, hum of the glass washer, and the pounding of Alvin's heart the only sounds. He opened the bag and saw stacks of cash, all in fifties. A rough count made more then enough to clear the debt owed. After inspecting some of the notes for forgery he dropped the stack back into the bag, leant back and sighed.

It was as if he'd been wearing a heavy back pack and someone had taken it off him. He felt lighter, freer, even giddy. Leaving the glasses on the table Alvin went to the bar, hid the cash under the counter, and poured a large glass of best whiskey. With a splash of cold water he absently swirled the mix, thinking. Anger welled at Colin. He felt betrayed at the thought of his daughter being used like some street whore. Downing the glass in one, hardly feeling the burn as it went down, Alvin made his choice. No more would the 4power crew meet at the Bull. No more would he expose his only child to their kind of scum.

Smiling with relief Alvin poured another glass, and looking over the bar, his bar, now free from debt and fear. While his daughter snored loudly above, dreaming the dreams of the shamed and broken, Alvin toasted his good fortune.

13

Christie came down stairs late, bleary eyed. The bar was still a mess, some drunks snoring loudly. Fear gripped her. Her dad never left it this bad. Eyes darting to the till only made her feel worse. The cash drawer was open, the black plastic tray missing. Unsure whether or not to call out for her dad Christie crept around the bar, ears straining, eyes wide. The noise of drunken sleep and her own heart filled her world. The mid morning sun slanted through the gaps in the drawn curtains. The front door was wide open.

Christie was ready to call the police, evidence or not of something happening, when soft singing slipped into her ears. Taking the old golf club, a five iron, from behind the bar Christie held it like a baseball bat, over her right shoulder. She moved slowly, gingerly. Glasses were still spread out over the tables, some with wasps and flies drawn to the sweet alcohol. On one table was the plastic glass basket, half full. Feeling strangely calm Christie skirted tables, and the odd body, heading for the snug. A hunched man sat with his back to her at one table, the darkened room hiding his features. He seemed to still be very drunk. There was nobody else. In the gloom she saw the square shape of the cash tray, a carrier bag with what looked like money or wads of paper made to look like money, and her father's jacket. Adjusting her grip on the club Christie lifted the club and stepped softly into the snug. The man still sang quietly, happily, to himself. He seemed to be counting out stacks of notes, arraigning them into piles of random shapes. As she got closer Christie thought they looked like a small pyramid, square at the base, slowly growing to a flat point. The man was humming a tuneless melody, absorbed in his work. The pyramid was nearly built, the carrier bag empty, when the man ran out of stacks. Grunting in irritation he lifted the cash tray, emptying more stacks from the segmented trays.

"You better put that down and kiss your ass goodbye," Christie said, trying to sound tougher then she felt.

The man paused, tray in the air. Finally he spoke.

"You watch your mouth, young lady. I can still tan your behind you know."

At the voice Christie dropped the club and ran forwards. In the half light she finally recognised her dad, looking tired, aged, but with a new youthfulness underneath, like the soft apples under a layer of crumble.

He held her in his arms, in a grip so tight it hurt. His

body tensed and the tears began to flow. At last he let her go, and as she stood his hand flew, striking her cheek so hard she fell backwards.

"What the hell, Dad?" she shouted, holding her glowing face.

"You ever do that again," he dad said, standing over her, full of authority, "and I'll use a cane on your ass."

"Language, Daddy," she said unconsciously, feeling like a little girl.

"Language my arse," Alvin said. He sat back on the chair, backwards, so he faced her resting on the back. "I know."

"Know what?" asked Christie, standing.

"I know it all. Colin, that git, the blackmailing turd making you into his whore." Alvin grew angrier as he spoke, straining through clenched teeth. "I know how he made you do things, use your body to help me. It all makes sense now. Bastard." He spat the last word out, fists clenched.

Christie knelt before him, her soft hands over his. "Daddy, I didn't do it for him, well, maybe to start with. But afterwards I did it for me. I knew he had you in his little web. The debts, the lies, the control he had over you. I didn't want that. I wanted my dad back."

Alvin looked her in the eye. "Did you sleep with the kid?"

A tear fell from her eye. "Yes, dad."

Her fathers hands tightened under hers, his body firming as if ready for a fight.

Looking up at her father she said "but I wanted to. Not for Colin, not for the pub, not even for you. I love him, dad."

The old man's eyes searched, darting back and forth. After a breathless moment his body relaxed.

"The problems are gone, our debt is paid," he said.

"How?" asked Christie.

Alvin spun around on the chair with some difficulty and pointed to the pyramid. Closer she saw it was money, stacks of fifty pound notes, all in little paper collars like you get from the bank. She picked one up, thinking abstractly how heavy it was. Running a finger through like they do in the movies it made the same rustling noise, the smell of paper floating. Trying to count the notes her dad chuckled.

"There's over two hundred thousand here, all in fifties. Your man brought it over. It's near double what we need to pay back Colin."

Christie dropped the note on the pyramid, wiping her hands on her crumpled night shorts.

"Dad, it isn't stolen, you think?"

"You tell me. I never met the bugger before last night."

Christie suddenly felt panic again. Could Tez be a thief? He had the means of stealing this much. Without a word Christie ran upstairs to get changed.

When she came down her dad had tidied half the bar, run some glasses through the wash, and hidden the bag under the bar. He opened his mouth to speak but one raised finger stopped him. She ran through the still open door, squinting in the sun. Her car was still there, where she had parked it last night. The soft rumble of the large exhaust calmed her, but the knowledge the car had a lot of expensive parts in it only heightened the worry.

Stopping at his flat she saw the bike was gone. In the yard of the garage the other mechanics were busy, but old Hopdyke was there and he told her Tez had booked holiday.

"Strangest thing too," said the old man. "He called me at home last night, middle of the bloody night too. Said he had an emergency and had to go. He was due a break anyway, and deserved it too."

"Did he say where he was going, Mr Hopdyke?"

"Not to me, Missy. My guess is family." Hopdyke saw her car. "So it was for you he did the car? Fair play to him."

Christie looked puzzled, then realised. "Yeah, he did. Did he pay for it all himself?"

"Sure did. Said it was old winnings. Cost a pretty penny too. Never seen a man spend so much on a car. If it was for you, then it was worth it," he finished with a wink that made her back itch.

"Thanks," she said uneasily. "You know where his family live?"

"No idea. Quiet one that kid." He smiled knowingly. "I'm sure you want to 'thank' him for what he's done. My advise is wait two weeks. He'll be back, I'm sure."

Christie tried to smile. It came out more of a grimace. Thanking Hopdyke she left, going back to his flat. She knew the landlord lived at the end flat. Knocking his door she waited impatiently, shuffling from foot to foot.

"Wadda you want?" came an angry voice through the door.

"Ah, hi. I'm looking for Tez," she called back.

"Who?"

"Terrence, from 4a?"

"Ah, the kid with the bike? He's away. Back in a couple of weeks, but his place is secure so don't go breaking in."

Christie knew he could see her through the peep hole but couldn't stop a giggle.

"I know. If you see him tell him Christie wants to see him ASAP."

Yeah, whatever," the voice grunted. Heavy footsteps told her the conversation was over.

Feeling lost she sat outside Tez's door. She felt betrayed that he had left so quickly, insulted he hadn't said goodbye, and worried that this could be related to the money. If he had stolen it, then vanishing for two weeks was wise. Still, her dad was out of the red, her heart could wait a fortnight, and she had an awesome car to drive.

With a weight lifted she started to feel better. She tried calling his mobile phone for the tenth time, but still got straight to voice mail. Clicking her tongue in annoyance she got back into her car and went home.

The wind whistled around his helmet, the exhaust sang behind him and the sun cast his shadow ahead like a magnet. Tez felt happy. He had no idea where he was going, or for how long. He only knew he had to clear his head, and two weeks on the road alone was the only way he knew how. With no radio, no music, no phone and no distractions he was free to ride the country lanes away from town, leaving mental baggage in the verges as he went.

He had to skip town, only for a little while, to figure out what to do. He knew he loved Christine, he felt bad for her dad, and was only too happy to help. He knew he still wanted to be with her, even after all she had said. The feeling of love, the spark that becomes an all consuming inferno still blazed. What to do with it was what he needed to figure out. So he planned to ride until he was tired, find a hotel to sleep in until he wasn't tired, then ride again. With no destination apart from a clear head he sped on, letting the sun warm his back, and his mind clear the junk.

14

That afternoon Christie dropped her note at Colin's home, leaving it under his wiper blade. Expecting fireworks she went straight back to the pub, packing a small case into her car. Inside it was as normal, but Alvin had prepared himself, adding a long kitchen knife to the golf club behind the bar.
Christie sat in the kitchen, nursing a cold cup of strong tea.
The bar was empty.

As the sun began to head out for the night the unmistakable sound of a tuned car rumbled into the car park. Alvin stood, squeezing his daughters hand, and went out into the private area of the pub, leaving the back door ajar. Colin half ran through the open front door, didn't notice the lack of people or even Alvin behind the bar, and nearly took the kitchen door off it's hinges. He looked evil, full of anger and malice. He waved her note in one clenched hand.

"What the fuck is the meaning of this, bitch?" He thrust it in her face, Christie unintentionally shrinking back. "You think this is a game?"

"No," she managed, in a weak and scared voice. "I can't do it any more. I can't be a whore for you."

Colin slammed his hand on the wooden table, making the half full cup bounce. "Whore? You were always a whore. From the moment you were born you were made to be shafted for cash. Now you made a deal, or do you want me to claim back what your dad owes?"

Christie, through tears, shook her head. Colin took it for agreement.

"Good. So when that little prick comes back you crawl back to him."

Christie still shook her head, but she spoke with

conviction. "No, Colin. I won't. He's a good man, way better than you. I won't be a pawn in your stupid game. Say what you want, and I know you will, but you can't make me play your games any more."

Shocked Colin stared at her, rage burning his face crimson. "You what?!" He reached for her, but stopped. A cruel smile formed, more unnerving than the anger. "Well, I guess daddy will be looking for a new home then."

"No, he won't." Alvin pushed the door open, bag in one hand, club in the other. "You tried to play her like you did me, but guess what? You lose, ass hole. Here." Alvin dropped the bag on the table. Stacks of notes fell out in a slow slide.

Colin watched the money briefly, then looked incredulously at Alvin. "What the fuck? Where did you get that?"

"Money owed," said Alvin.

A change came over Colin. Slowly he seemed to calm, almost apologetic. "You didn't get a loan to pay me back? Silly. I wasn't charging interest. Now you just made things worse for yourself," he said, friendly, calm.

"I didn't get a loan," said Alvin, still calm, but in control. "This was owed by, well, by a friend. It's all you are owed. Even before you tried to pawn my own child."

Colin checked the money, piling it into equal stacks. "Not enough," he said eventually. "You owe me another ten thou. No deal." He pushed the money back to Christie, who watched with wide eyes.

"Deal, butt munch," said Alvin, ignoring the money. "You will accept it, you will bugger off my property and never come back. You and your boys are banned, for life. Find a new place to piss off."

Colin almost recoiled, putting a hand out to a counter

top to steady himself. "You don't mean that. What about our poker games? The money we spend here?"

Alvin took a step forwards, club lowered by his leg. "I do. I don't want your business, and I don't need it. I make more than enough, and your ass holes cost me more than they spend. And you, you little free loader, you drink half my profits by yourself. So now you can bugger off. So get!"

Alvin took another step forward, aiming to use his body to tell Colin to go. The cowered man took a step back, but his eyes changed, half closed, focused. Alvin realised his mistake too late, tried to raise the club, but Colin's fist was a blur. Alvin's head snapped back as if it were on a string and someone had yanked on it. Blood flowed in an arc from his nose. The fist blurred again, and again. Alvin staggered back, reeling. Christie screamed something and through squinting eyes Alvin saw her bent double as a fist hit her gut, then almost comically fly backwards as another struck her face. The face of the monster, eyes narrow slits, teeth bared, nostrils wide, turned back on him. As the fist pumped his face and body the last thought Alvin had was at least it wasn't his daughter getting hit, then the world greyed to black.

Panting, arms aching, Colin looked at the old man on the floor. His fists stung, even when the hard skull softened under his relentless knuckles. Fearing the man may die Colin grabbed the home phone and dialled 999. When asked which service he spoke in a high falsetto voice for an ambulance. Once done he left, smashing the CCTV recorder before he did. Christie was out cold on the floor. The punch to her belly had winded her, but the one to her face had sent her flying into the fridge, making everything hurt, then go dark. When she woke there was a man in a white shirt with green letters leaning over with a small torch.

He seemed miles away, looking down a long tunnel.

"This one's gonna be ok, but some serious head injury. Best get her down to A&E fast, just to be sure."

"What about the man?" asked another voice, out of sight of the tunnel.

"Doubtful," said the first, noticing Christie was waking up.

"Hey. I'm Paul, a paramedic. You feeling ok?"

Christie tried to speak, but nothing worked. Her head pounded like the world's worst hangover, her neck was made of stone. She tried to wave a hand, but moving sent fire up her back into her brain. The man shushed her, putting a plastic collar on her neck. Into view came more men in shirts, carrying a small bed. Her vision was widening. She saw it was a hospital type bed used in ambulances. She was going to hospital. Why? She was fine.

The men stood around her like bearers around a coffin. The first man was saying something about moving her, but the words were drowned by the bass thump in her head. When they rolled her onto her side to put the bed under she gave a gasp as the pain flared, then darkness came, cool, painless dark.

Tez had stopped at a motel near eighty miles from home. It wasn't much, but it was comfy, had wifi and a decent café next door. He'd been there a couple of days, rebooking the room each morning. The girl behind the counter in the café was cute, and obviously liked him, given the extra bacon and hash browns on his breakfast plate. She didn't look anything like Christine though, and that hurt. He was trying to decide what to do, but there was so much going on around him. He could stay and make a life with her, knowing the past, or leave and run again. If he stayed he'd have to tell his past, no better than hers. If he ran it was another new town, a new job and a new life and that took a lot of effort. He liked Lower Hampton. There were better places, he was sure. But that old town had life, feeling, and Christine. The bars were few and far between, the ugly new retail park a beauty spot on the towns face, but it had a sense of history, of continuity. He felt as close to being at home there as he had ever felt, even when he lived in the family home. There they accepted him as another travelling stranger, hoping to set roots down, but ready to up and leave too. He felt almost accepted, needed, wanted. Hopdyke may be an old fool, but he knew Tez's value and took care of him. Henderson may be a wannabe tough copper, a guy who wanted a career no matter what. But that didn't bother Tez. He had, and could still handle him. There was plenty of money in the bag still, and plenty of life left in him to make more. The gangs bothered him most.

He knew that without him they would keep going, but if they got him, especially his car, then the results would be a disaster. He had heard enough about the Hopwood men to know he didn't want to be caught between the two, but caught he was. Now he had to figure out not only how to get himself out of trouble, but Christie too.

Ignoring the cute waitress's almost doting stare Tez chomped his cooked breakfast, watching the small TV mounted on the wall. The news was on, he was waiting for the weather so he could plan the day. Headlines were uninteresting. A fire in California, earthquakes and cheating politicians as usual. The local news was next and the head line froze his heart. With a fork full of beans stalled on the way to his mouth he saw the Black Bull pub, surrounded by police cars, blue tape over the front door. Christine's pink car was parked to one side. A young man was speaking to the camera calmly.

"Yesterday afternoon a horrific attack on this public house behind me has left one young woman with serious head wounds, and her father in intensive care. Police as yet have no leads on who committed this terrible attack, or why. The bar was open with no customers or witnesses. The security cameras were disabled, however no money was taken. Police are suspecting it was an attempted burglary, interrupted by the landlord and his daughter, who were assaulted, before the thieves fled. Police are asking anyone with information to contact Inspector Henderson at Lower
Hampton police station immediately. Back to the studio."

The TV played to an empty table. Tez was already running to his bike, clawing for his keys.

15

The constricting smell of cleaning solution, the odour of disinfectant, food and clean fabrics stuck in Tez's throat like a summer cold. Around him the room was silent save the beep of machines, his own breathing, and the passing sound of footsteps. Tez was by nature a typical male, preferring to hide emotions instead of reacting how he felt. However, seeing Christine in that bed, hooked up to monitors, pipes sticking out all over the place, face swollen completely out of shape, made the tears flow unbidden. She had been well and truly battered. The doctors had said she would recover, and have little physical affects, but the hit on her head from a counter had cracked her skull on the crown, giving her a small brain bleed. They had operated, but she still slept, not waking even as he held her hand to shaking lips. Now he sat numbly, watching her chest rise and fall in the thin hospital gown, the only sign of life.

The door opened and closed softly behind him. In the impressively uncomfortable hospital chair Tez ignored it, thinking it only a nurse doing their checks. Instead a shadow passed, and the familiar face of Inspector Henderson passed him without a word and sat on the other side of the bed, first looking out the window, then to the sleeping form.

"Amazing, really," Henderson said. Tez kept silent. The inspector shook his head, leant back, one leg crossed over the other. "The human body can take a hell of a beating and keep going. Still, she'll get better."

Tez tensed his hand into a fist, covered with the other. Last thing he really wanted was this pompous copper preaching to him now.

Henderson leant forwards, looking at Tez. "You know who did it?" he asked.

Tez didn't look back, just shook his head.

"You have any idea?" Henderson sounded almost passive, as if he didn't really care. Tez shrugged his shoulders.

Henderson stood, and leant on the wall, looking through the window. "I know who you are, kid. I know what you did, and what you can do. I know she was your bit of fluff, and I know you were seeing her a lot. I know her dad owed that tosser Hopwood, and I figured you paid it off." Henderson turned to face Tez, who finally looked up with red eyes. "I also know who did this."

Tez stood, with a face that nearly made Henderson step back involuntarily. That face could scare a serial killer.

Face to face, kissing distance, Tez spoke softly. "Who?"

Henderson forced a smile. "You know. See, kid, I know a lot about this town. I also know the history, something you won't. Now, I can tell you, but that means shit, as I can't prove it. No evidence, so no official stand."

Tez still squared off to the stockier man like a boxer in the ring. The smile on the inspectors face faded.

"All I want is to clean the crap from this town, get the scum out so I can move on." Henderson sat back down, leaving Tez to intimidate the wall. "Maybe, if we worked together, we could both get what we want."

"All I want is my life, her life, and that bastard's head firmly rammed up his own arse," said Tez.

"I'll bet. Seriously though, I can't encourage anything, well, illegal. I can accidentally drop hints, and be ready to send in the blue troops if hints are dropped back."

Tez knew what he was saying, the hints dropping like hailstones. He sat back down, still tensed, only softening when he looked at Christine's distorted face.

"So drop your hints," he said.

Henderson crossed his legs, and played with his phone. "Now you know I can't do that," he said.

"If you want to play games with people bugger off and find some other git to play with, before I stuff that phone up your arse sideways."

Henderson smiled, almost laughed. "Now, now, kid. No need to get upset. I told you, history. Someone with a bad temper, someone who plays to win, someone," he leant forwards, voice dropped to near a whisper, "someone who wants everything his way, and everything to be his."

The inspector saw the young man's face firm, lips pressed together, and knew he understood. The cheeks quivered as the teeth clenched, and those hazel eyes grew colder and darker. Tez stood, and went to leave.

"You won't get near him, though," Henderson said, absently.

Tez paused, hand on the big door handle.

"He's got his mates, his stupid gang around him. You try to do anything and they'll bury you," Henderson continued. "You wanna take him out? You gotta be smart. Play him at his own game. You walk in there guns blazing they will shoot you down, literally. You sneak in they'll catch you, and we may find some bits of you when they start to really stink. You ain't dumb, you have brains that are wasted. Use them. Use them properly."

Henderson fell silent. Sensing the conversation was over Tez took a breath and left.

With the loss of the Bull the 4power crew met instead outside McDonald's in the retail area. They couldn't drink, and the staff were more than a little intimidated by the massive crowd of noisy cars, thumping speakers, and skimpy outfits. Parents passed them, using the drive through at Burger King next door instead. Marked police cars cruised past, but didn't do anything more than slow down as they passed. The smell of tyre smoke, weed and burgers hung like a cloud. Lights flashed, people chatted, and some went to add to the growing lines of black burnt rubber on the tarmac.

Colin leant against his Skyline, absently checking out the women. Hot pants so short you saw ass cheeks, and under boob tops seemed to be the latest style, with massive hoop earrings, a lot of make up and blonde hair dye. Not that he minded. He kept up his chats with passing members, mostly Martin. Everyone noticed the black leather fingerless gloves Colin wore, but knew well enough to keep silent. Some even ordered similar gloves on line, to keep up with their leader.

"So, we all good for the grudge match next month?"

asked Colin.

"Yeah, I guess," said Martin, staring at one leggy brunette with shorts that looked more like a thong.

"You guess?"

Martin snapped back to the conversation. Colin was looking at him funny, questioning.

"Yeah, we're good. Got everything tweaked and checked. Been down last weekend to check the track. Not been used, so no chance of being accused of cheating." Martin made a weak smile that bounced off Colin like a ricocheting bullet.

"We better. This year it's our year, I feel it." Colin leant on the car, elbows resting on the roof so he looked like a reclining tyrannosaurus. "What about the tit with the fast car? Found it yet?"

"Not yet, Colin. Had a few guys looking, but the kid skipped town. Found out he came home this morning. Went straight to the hospital."

Colin chuckled, absently massaging his knuckles through the gloves. "Ah, yes. How is our favourite filly and her dad?"

Martin shrugged. "Word is she'll be fine. Small bleed on the brain, been operated on. Doubt she'll be up for a couple of weeks. Her dad ain't too good." Martin dropped his voice and leant closer. "Colin, man, you really went too far. The guy may die, actually die. He's critical, brain injury, multiple broken bones, ruptured organs. You really did go too far."

Colin shook his head with a dismissive wave. "Piss off. How the hell those knobs gonna know it was me? They have nothing on me." He half turned, shoulders hunched, making Martin flinch. "And if no twat goes around saying things they will never know, got it?"

Martin knew that tone, cold and promising. He nodded,

keeping his mouth firmly closed.

Colin smiled and gently slapped Martin's cheek. "Good. Now, let's go have some fun, eh?" Colin went for the brunette, grabbing her ass and when she spun to slap him he bent her over like a ballroom dancer does a perfect dip, and kissed her. Martin shook his head, but smiling he followed.

Unseen from behind a closed shop near the restaurant Tez watched, and waited.

As the night grew old the group broke up slowly. Some had work, others family to see to. Most of the girls stayed, some hoping for some action, most for a race or two. After midnight Colin led the remaining cars out. Tez followed at a distance, easily keeping track of the loud exhausts and neon lights. They passed the Black Bull, still closed up, and headed into the countryside south of the town. Turning down a narrow lane Tez saw on the left an old abandoned wartime runway. The group passed the grass and concrete landing strip, with the old control tower standing guard, and headed deeper into the dark country lanes. About three miles from town, and a mile past the runway, Colin stopped the group. Here was a straight piece of road between a line of trees.

Sending two cars down to the end Colin walked from car to car, pausing briefly to speak to the driver, then going to the next. As the first two cars lined up Tez realised they were drag racing, using the long straight for practice. The first two revved their engines, exhausts popping. One of the girls raised both arms in her very short top, smiled, then dropped to the floor. Both cars vanished into a cloud of tyre smoke, appearing ten metres down the road accelerating fast.

Tez hid his bike behind a hedge in a farmers field, using

a piece of wood to stop the side stand sinking in the soft grass, then crept along the hedgerow until he was close enough to hear words clearly.

"I know it," said a voice. "I know I gotta beat Midge and his Jap crap Honda. But until someone sorts that crappy fuel map I can't beat a bloody push bike."

Tez tried to peek through the hedge. Nearest him was a blue Nissan Pulsar. One guy, most likely the driver, was leaning with an arm on the open bonnet while another had his head buried in the engine bay.

"Look, can't you do anything?" asked the standing man.

"Not really," said the one in the engine. "See, your map is fine. It's this crappy wiring you got here." The man stood and pointed. "See this? Shit. There is no way that can take the load you need. And by the way, your turbo is dead. I heard it rattle when you pulled up. You need a new one, boost pipe, waste gate and put some decent leads on for fucks sake."

The engine man turned and walked away in anger. The driver, still leaning on his bonnet muttered under his breath and slammed it closed.

Beside the Nissan was an old Mazda RX7 made out like a drift car. It was empty, but behind one guy was sat on the low, wide boot, head back, almost looking asleep. Tez shifted to get a better look and saw a head with long blonde hair bobbing rhythmically below his waist. Trying to keep silent Tez ignored the couple, and kept going down the line. The road was narrow, but a large farm gateway and the entrance to a power substation provided parking for all the cars side by side. This meant Tez could pass behind half of them, but not all. The chain link fence stopped him after a green RS Focus next to the Mazda.

Trying to see around the large rear of the Ford Tez could just about see the back end of Colin's dark Skyline.

He couldn't hear anything over the sound of revving engines, loud music, and laughter. Tez was about to try and go around the substation when he heard footsteps. Crouching low to the ground, knowing the hedge was thinner near the fence he saw the man from the Mazda, flies still undone, walk towards him. Feeling his heart pound Tez kept low, like a rabbit, hoping the man would walk past. He didn't. The feet, in Addidas trainers, stopped behind the green Ford, right in front of Tez. Daring to look up he saw the man fish inside his open jeans. Knowing what that meant Tez wriggled away before the stream of hot fluid passed through the hedge. Tez was about to head back to his bike when he heard the engines stop and Colin raised his voice.

"Alright, listen you ass holes. You know we got a month to the grudge match. You all need to sort your cars. Tiny? You fix that turbo, right? Steve? You know that stuff so you help him. We work together people. Those twats have been doing my head in for too long now. This is our year."

"What about Mark and his bike? Hell of a bit of kit," said a voice.

Tez tried to see around, but the Focus was blocking his view. Avoiding the puddle he leant near the fence, ears straining.

"Don't worry about my brother," Colin said, spitting the word 'brother' out like poison. "I got a plan for that cheating bastard."

"Your first one didn't work," replied the voice.

There was a scuffle of feet, some heads appeared around the Ford as people moved.

"That's because that dozy bitch couldn't seduce a fucking dildo," Colin said, low and dangerous. "Now we go to plan bloody B."

The voice stayed silent, the mood changed to tension.

"Now then," said Colin, addressing them all again. "We have only a few more weekends to prep and tune so use tonight to practice your starts, find the weak parts and replace them."

The engines started and Tez headed back to his bike. He was covered from the knees down in mud and leaves, but finding a space where there was a gap in the hedge he crawled through and watched the racing. He was too far to hear anything, but he didn't mind. He just waited for it to end. An hour later it did, Colin gathering them together and leading them out. Tez was shivering in his wet jeans, but he pulled his bike out of the field and followed.

Heading back to town past the Bull the convoy turned left into the council area of town. Here were small terraced homes for low income and some larger semi detached for the bigger families. It was harder to follow the cars without getting too close, but luckily for Tez the council had done as most do and made the streets into a wavy grid, so if he missed a turn he could follow on the next. Finally the engines stopped and Tez hid his bike behind a large van, putting his helmet and jacket under it to hide them. The cars had parked outside a larger semi, Colin's Skyline and Martin's Audi RS4 were on the drive. Music blared even though it was three in the morning. Nobody yelled out for them to turn it down, and no police were called. Tez guessed this happened a lot, and everyone knew to keep quiet.

The shadows on the drawn curtains downstairs showed a party was in full swing. Arms held bottle silhouettes to outlined faces, feminine arms were held over heads as they swayed to the heavy bass beats. The kitchen on the side was lit, but no blinds drawn. Using a neighbours car

as cover Tez managed to get close enough to see inside.
Martin was leaning on the cooker, brown beer bottle in
hand. Several cardboard crates were stacked by the door.
Two girls were kissing passionately while the men cheered
and watched. Colin was nowhere to be seen.

Tez couldn't get closer, and as the night lightened into
day he knew the others were going nowhere. Irritated
he'd missed his chance Tez crept back to his bike, pulled
his jacked and helmet on and rode home.

16

Deciding against going back to work Tez instead used
the time following Colin and his group. He mapped out
their home, work and meet addresses, and who was
where and when. As he left one house with a 4power car
outside he noticed the sound of motorbike engines going
fast. As he looked around for the source five bikes
surrounded him, one giving a 'come here' gesture with a
gloved finger. In the centre of the pack he had little
choice but to follow.

They rode fast and close, sometimes almost touching
each other. Tez had to admit they were amazing riders,
getting as close as track racers on the rough narrow
streets. He also noticed the Yoki Rider logo on their bikes
and leathers, and guessed this was not a social invite.
Trapped in the group he couldn't escape without
knocking one of them off their bike and probably doing
the same to himself so he allowed himself to be led.

They took him north, past the main street with the
garage and the market place, and towards the dual
carriage way. Before they had passed the new build area

they turned left into a familiar yard. Tez had seen Crippin's Motorcycle Shop before, a great local place for parts and tyres. Now he was escorted into the yard around the side where at least thirty bikes lined two sides. The escort bikers peeled off and blocked the exit, while the others just leant on their bikes, looking uninterested. Tez stopped in the middle, flicked the kill switch and waited.

One man eventually got off his bike and started walking towards Tez. He was skinny under his leather trousers, a vest top showed little muscle on his arms, and the dark ponytail made him look like an '80's yuppie from an American film. As he got closer Tez saw the lines of scars on his right shoulder. Surgical scars.

The man stopped a few feet away, and tilted his head. Tez realised he wanted him to remove his helmet, and did so, resting it on the bikes tank.

"Thank you," said the man. Tez nodded back. Everyone was silent, engines off, as they waited. The man smiled briefly and looked at the floor. "Your bike?" he asked.

"I'm sat on it," said Tez, feeling more than a little confused.

"True. Don't think you remember me," the man said. Tez finally clicked when he spoke. It was the man from the garage, the brother of Colin. He saw the realisation on Tez's face and smiled again. "Thought we should have another little chat." Mark waved an arm for Tez to follow, and went to sit on a picnic bench by the shop. Tez reluctantly followed, still trying to figure out what was going on.

Mark offered a bottle of beer, that Tez wasn't surprised to see was Corona, and when it was he refused a can of Iron Bru was produced instead. As Tez opened the can Mark took a swig and sighed.

"My brother has caused a lot of problems over the years, and hurt a lot of people. I know you liked the Thorpe girl, and I'm sorry. Sometimes I wish I knew where his anger comes from. Anyway, I also know you wanna get back at him, and I don't blame you. I won't even stop you. All I ask is one thing."

He paused and Tez felt the pull to fill the void of words. Instead he sipped noisily at his can. Mark saw he wasn't going to answer and smiled again. This smile was warmer, kinder than his brother's evil grimace. It was almost brotherly.

"All I ask is you don't kill him. He may be an ignorant arse hole, but he is my brother."

Tez drained the can, throwing his head back, checking quickly as he did. There was nobody behind him. He put the empty can on the bench, hands to his sides.

"He nearly killed Christie, and may have killed her dad. I feel for you, but unless he decides to stand still and be clobbered I will batter him, and I ain't gonna stop until I choose to." Tez raised one hand, balled it into a fist, and slammed it onto the can, neatly flattening it into a disc. Mark looked from the can to Tez, then back to the can. He fingered the small ring in the wooded bench almost regretfully.

"I see. All I ask is to keep that in mind." Mark leant back and looked Tez in the face. Tez looked back. Everyone watched the silent battle as both weighed each other up.

Mark broke first, smiling, and reaching for another bottle.

"You know I gotta do it?" asked Tez, ignoring an offered can of pop.

"Yeah, I guess I do. My brother is a great guy, you may not see it, may not realise, but he is."

"Like Hitler," said Tez without humour.

Mark shot him a pained look. "Maybe, but he does a lot of good too. He has raised thousands for charity, he kept the Bull in business, and…"

"That's crap," shouted Tez, making Mark jump. "He cheated that poor guy at cards, then blackmailed him to get his own way. And when Alvin stood up to him, your saintly brother damn near killed him. Yeah, he's a freaking angel."

Mark still held the pained smile. "I never said he was perfect, but he has a good side. Bit buried perhaps, but good. It's just his temper. He always had it, even as a kid. He'd get into fights, say the wrong thing, fly off in rage. I'd always calm him down."

"So what happened then? He turn on you too?"

Mark drained his nearly full bottle, stood, and took Tez gently by the elbow. He led him past everyone and out to a narrow alley running behind the shop. He leant against the shops back wall and sighed. Tez waited, eyes darting, just in case.

"My brother is my brother," said Mark. "I love him as you would love your kin. It's just his temper. I had to fight it all my life. My parents had to face it, but I had to fight it. It's like someone intent on drowning, you gotta keep pulling them back up. I got tired. One day I just broke." Mark looked at his scuffed bike boots, idly pushing dirt into a pile. "He wanted a race. We did it a lot. I always raced bikes, Colin cars. When we got back we found our sister Samantha had been in a crash. We'd promised to look at her car, the brakes were a bit soft. But we went out racing instead."

Tez leant on the wooden fence opposite, trying to read the man before him, keeping silent. Mark built his pile higher.

"Dad was mightily pissed of course. Mum was crying.

We all went to the hospital, but it was too late. Colin just stormed out, damn near took the door with him. We all stood around that bed in hospital, numb, you know?"

Mark didn't look up, but he knew Tez was thinking about Christie, lying in her metal framed bed on wheels. The dust pile grew wider.

"I went after him. I knew his temper and didn't want him blowing his safety valve on anyone. Instead he blew on me. In the car park he was raging. I tried to calm him, but he turned on me. Blamed me. Said it was my fault we went racing instead of looking at her car. Maybe it was, but not just me. Now I know it was grief that made him like that, and me. But I turned on him. We both lost some blood, some pride, a couple of teeth, and our brotherhood. He left, walking home. I wasn't able to walk, but at least I was already at the hospital. Now we ain't kin, just two guys."

Tez saw the pile, now with a flat top, was hit by two small, wet meteors, leaving craters.

"Hey, I know the feeling. My folks hate me too."

Mark looked up, wet eyes. "My parents don't hate me. We talked, later. They said she shouldn't have used the car. We had others. Hell, we had three. She just loved that car. Police said the brakes were weak, not good enough to stop in an emergency. A lorry ran a red light. She probably couldn't have stopped in time anyway." Mark shrugged, looking back down at his small mountain.

Tez looked at the clouds, high and white. "Maybe. But she didn't. Why the wars?"

"Wars? Well, Colin wanted everything. Claimed he owned all this. We used to ride together, bikes and cars. In the evenings we'd race in the hills, then later go for a drink at the Smelters Arms, opposite the cop shop."

"Nice place," said Tez, who'd been in a couple of times

with workmates as his socialising increased.

"Yeah, it is. Not been in since we fell out. Now Colin wants the whole town, says he started all this, and it belonged to him. He hates bikes now. Says they're death traps and anyone on one is nothing but an organ donor. His lot followed like sheep, and this ain't a big town. Eventually it came to blows. Papers did a big spread, that tit Henderson came in, and we drew up a division. Now we race for what we lost, or what we want. Grudge matches."

Tez looked down from the clouds. "Grudge matches?"

"Yeah. Once a year, down the old airstrip."

"Ah, yeah. Heard about them," said Tez, thinking.

Mark kicked his dirt pile, fanning the dust. "Well, it's a month away, and I know he's desperate to win this year."

"Your brother?" asked Tez.

"Yep. He wants your car. I know that."

"How?"

Mark smiled. He almost looked back to normal. "Just because we're fighting, that doesn't mean everyone is. Most of my lot want to rejoin, and I think his do too. We talk, we share, hell we meet up occasionally. I heard Colin wants your car to beat me. Got my new bike last year, too late to race, but now he knows he won't win."

"And what do you get for winning?" asked Tez.

"Whatever you bet."

"And what would he bet?"

Mark laughed. "The whole damn town. He wants the bikes out."

"But if his guys like bikes, why don't they just say?"

The laugh died. "Scared. He rules with fear. He never learnt social skills, but he knows how to manipulate. They wouldn't dare leave, but they don't want it to stay this way."

"And if he wins?"

Mark sighed. He went back to building another pile. "He will get rid of every guy in my lot. Banned from riding, racing, everything."

"And if you win?" asked Tez.

"He drops his stupid feud," Mark smiled. "And comes home."

"You live at home? With your family?"

"Yeah. Family matters. We all just want him to come home."

Tez paused. He felt a little shaken. He hadn't thought of anywhere but where he kicked off his shoes as home. Now he felt homesick for his folks, even his bratty sister.

"One last ask," said Tez. Mark looked up to meet his gaze. "What if someone outside wanted to race?" "Do they have a grudge?" asked Mark.

"I think they might."

Mark laughed again, making Tez feel warmth towards him, like he wanted to have another drink with this guy, and damn it he will.

"Well then, tell your 'friend' to be there three weeks Saturday at half eight in the morning. And be ready. It's not a simple race."

"As in?" asked Tez.

"As in it comes in three parts. Drag, circuit and a final precision part." Mark saw the look in the outsider's face and was already planning.

"Maybe," said Tez, "you could explain over a little drink?
All this chat's making my mouth dry."

"Mine too," said Mark, putting an arm over Tez's shoulders and leading him back inside.

17

The grudge races were indeed in three stages. Stage one was a drag race, two a circuit and three was a precision race around markers laid out. The length and level of each race was set by the challenger, and all calls had to be made at the start, with details on each race when the challenge is made. If accepted there's no backing out, and the loser has to pay up there and then, no 'double or quits'. The drag was a simple drag race, over a predefined distance with one person at the start and one at the end with radios to say the results. All matches are done together, so all the drag races are done before the circuits begin. Bets on races by non competitors are allowed on the same pay up basis.

The two groups are kept apart, with the racers lining up in order of seniority. Colin and Mark race last on each event. For Tez's plan to work he'd need to be there early, and he'd need his car perfect. He decided not to go back to work. Instead, having his second week off, he would spend more time on prep. After seeing Mark he rode to the airstrip. Club members were strictly banned from practising on the strip to make it fairer, but Tez wasn't affiliated, so he could cheat all he wanted. He rode the old concrete following the tyre marks still faintly etched on the surface. The strip was used sometimes by amateur pilots and gliders so was in decent condition. Ignoring the looks a few late fliers gave him Tez mapped out the circuit and the grip on the drag strip. Having made his assessment of the track he went home and drew up a plan so he could map it in his head.

Sunday he went to visit Christie in hospital. She was a

lot better. Her face was more or less its original shape, the dark smudge of bruises still there. She looked strange without make up, her hair unkempt. Barely awake she smiled when he came in, holding her arms out like a child, tears brimming. He held her tight, making the nurse on her ward smile when they both rocked side to side. Finally they broke apart.

"Hey you," said Tez, kissing her.

"Hey you back," said Christie, yawning.

"How you feeling?"

"You know," she replied, shrugging. "Get some wicked headaches. They say it'll ease off over time, but still kills. What about you?"

Tez sat in the vinyl hospital chair, ignoring the deathlike wheeze it made. "Not much," he said.

She gave him a look only a mother could give, the look that said 'I know you're lying'.

He stood and walked to the window. A familiar car parked in the doctors' designated parking spaces. "Be right back," Tez called out as he shot out the door.

He met Henderson as the inspector was getting into a lift.

"Hey, copper," he shouted.

Henderson stopped half in the lift, then turned and stepped back. The doors rolled closed behind him.

"Mr Belkin. You here for your girl?"

Tez walked up to him, took his arm and near dragged the man away. They stopped at the small hospital café where Tez got him a coffee and doughnut. Henderson held back a smile at the doughnut joke, but sipped the coffee.

"Well?" he asked.

Tez leant back, spun the cap of a bottle of Fanta and took a swig.

"Well," Tez replied.

"Why are you here buying me coffee?" asked Henderson.

"You like it here?" Tez said.

"A hospital caff? Not really my idea of a holiday spot."

Tez smiled. "I meant this town, this job you have?"

Henderson put the cheap ceramic mug down. "Now listen, son. If you want to make threats…"

"Me? No. but I know when the Hopwood thing is sorted you'll be moving on, right?"

"Yeah, if it gets sorted." Henderson resumed sipping the dark coffee.

"I think it may," said Tez.

Henderson looked at the young man over his cup. "Really? What makes you think that?"

Tez leant back, took another drink and smiled childishly. "Well, the grudge match is coming up soon, ain't it?"

"And?" asked Henderson, feeling irritated.

"And if Colin loses the gangs will end and peace will return to this happy town," said Tez, waving his arms theatrically.

"And if Colin wins it goes to hell," said Henderson.

"True. But what if someone, an outsider say, were to win?"

Henderson put down the cup, and held his hands over it in an arch. He searched the pleasantly smiling face for lies, for deceit, and Tez let him look. Without breaking contact Henderson said "Who?"

"Someone we both know, someone local, but decent," Tez answered.

"I don't know him, do I?"

"Maybe," said Tez, swirling the orange drink absently. "But maybe he could help you get out, back to the big city. If you could say there was a definite peace here, a permanent end to hostilities, that counts as a win?"

"A big win, yes. But how does that happen?"

Tez smiled, finished his bottle, screwed the cap back on and managed to throw it in the bin from fifteen feet. "Just be waiting for my signal. I'll let you know." He stood and left. Henderson watched him go, feeling small affection for the swaggering young man. He almost seemed a younger version of himself. He left the half drunk coffee and headed back to his car.

When Tez got back to the small cubicle Christie was waking having napped since he left. She was still slow, groggy. Her eyes were red, bags underneath. She looked like a healthy zombie. After blinking a few times she saw him looking back at her, expectantly. For a brief, unpleasant moment she looked almost confused, then a relieved smile split her face, lighting her eyes up. Tez smiled back, worry falling like an avalanche.

"Hey," she tried to say, voice croaking.

"Hey," he replied. He took the plastic water jug and poured the lukewarm water into the scratched plastic cup. She tried to sit up, but couldn't manage. He passed her the cup, letting her sip the water while she never took her eyes off him.

"Thanks," she said, a little more human. "What happened anyway?"

Tez opened his mouth to speak, then closed it. He pressed the call button for a nurse and tried to look calm. "Never you mind that. How do you feel?"

She pulled a face. "Like I just went on a weekend bender. My head is pounding." Her childish faces, like a little girl eating something that tasted nasty, made Tez worry. A nurse came in, pressing the button to stop the bell.

"Ah, young lady, how are we today?" the nurse asked in a friendly, happy voice.

"Don't know. What happened?" said Christie.

"Well, the doctor can explain all," said the nurse tactfully, checking her machine readouts, then she left. Christie gave Tez an enquiring look.

"What happened?" she asked slowly and deliberately.

Tez looked at the floor, torn between her feelings and her emotions. Finally he spoke. "You don't remember the fight?"

"Fight?"

Tez sighed, leant back in the chair and looked at the ceiling. Slowly he explained what he had heard on the news, filling in with his ideas of what happened. Christie's face went from shock, to anger, and finally tears as she thought of her father. She tried to get up but Tez stopped her, and the doctor arrived in perfect timing to help him.

"Now then, Ms Thorpe, you had a nasty experience, but you are well on the mend. Can you remember who you are?"

She gave him a really dirty look. "I'm not stupid, just feel like crap." She tried to sit up, visibly shook as her balance went, and fell back down. She put her hand over her eyes and groaned. "Why is the room spinning?" she asked.

The doctor held her wrist gently, looking at the monitors beside her bed. "You had a serious impact to the back of your skull, resulting in a minor fracture and some slight bleeding. We managed to stop the bleed, but you will feel imbalanced and discomfort for a few weeks. We had to sedate you to save you the risk of further injury." He kept looking at the monitors, then took a pen light and shone it in her eyes. Satisfied he nodded. "I think you will be able to go home in a couple of weeks, but no driving or heavy machinery for a couple of months until the headaches clear."

"You gonna go after him? After Colin?" she asked, ignoring the doctor, who wrote in her chart.

Tez nodded. "I don't fight much in life, not much worth getting angry over. But people matter, and you especially. This whole dumb war thing needs to end, and if you can be caught up in it I will end it. For you, and your dad."

"Doctor," she said, gripping his wrist with surprising strength. "My father. How is he?"

The doc looked to Tez for a moment, then looked back. You could almost see the cogs turn.

"You father was very badly hurt in the attack. He is still unconscious, and on the critical list. He's in intensive care at the moment. I can't say if he will ever wake again, or how he will be if he does."

Christie looked numbly at the doctor, eyes filling. She laid her head back on the pillow, tears flowing to her ears, staring at the ceiling. Tez thought she would burst into hysterics, but she lay quietly, blank faced. The doctor gently took her hand off his arm and laid it beside her on the blanket, gave the monitors one last check, and left, nodding to Tez.

Tez sat on the chair beside the bed feeling lost. Christie was reacting strangely to the news of her dad, he didn't know what to do and how to help her. If she had been crying he could have comforted her, were she angry he would calm her. This neutral reaction threw him. Hesitantly he stood, sat on the edge of the bed, laid his head on her chest, and tried to cuddle up to her. He heard her breathing, slow and deep. Her heart beat in his ears in time with the monitor. He closed his eyes, and held her tight, feeling the need for her support even though he should be supporting her. She ignored him, then laid one hand on his back, and the other stroked his short hair. After a long few minutes her chest started to heave and the tears fell quickly, her face screwed up as she cried openly. Tez held on to the bucking bronco as she let out her emotions. After a while he felt the queasiness of motion sickness.

18

Henderson parked in the lay-by on the dual carriageway again, waiting. He took a bottle of mineral water from the large centre cubby box and waited. The familiar loud exhaust of the RX8 pulled alongside. Henderson opened his window to the late summer evening.

"Well?" asked the voice from the small car.

Henderson waited, sipping his water.

"You got me out here for nothing?" asked the voice, getting angry.

"You know what I want to hear," said Henderson.

"Not really. I told you all I know."

Henderson shook his head, capped the water bottle and put it back in the box. "You do. I know Colin beat the crap out of Thorpe, I know he has used violence, blackmail and theft to try and wage a gang war. And I know you know too. So I can arrest you as an accessory, or when this all falls down I can turn a blind eye as you run away. Your choice."

The Mazda was silent. Henderson could wait for his answer. This guy had been his main source of info on the club, and he knew he had the kid by the balls. What he said was true, and he had played an ace card. He had told the kid the end was soon. Although the kid probably knew, now he knew that Henderson did too.

"So what do you want?" the kid asked eventually.

"I wanna know the date of the race, the line up and if anyone else joins in."

"Anyone else?"

Henderson looked into the dark interior of the race tuned Mazda. "An outsider."

Silence followed. A few cars passed, taking no notice of the large SUV parked beside the ground hugging sports car.

"Ok," said the kid. "Usual number?"

"Still got it," said Henderson.

"That all?"

"When it all comes down you will walk, or rather drive, away as fast as possible." Henderson took a small envelope from the passenger seat and tossed it through the open window. "If needs be that is a 'get out of jail free' card. You give me what I want we will let you go. You cross me, or lie, and I will make sure you never sit in a car again."

The Mazda's window rolled up, engine started, and left in a cloud of tyre smoke. Henderson watched the red tail lights go and smiled. That kid was a waste of space, but a small fish who could slip the net, maybe. Tez was his secret ace, and if he could bring the whole crap pile down, so much the better. Then Henderson could sweep in and clean the whole lot up in one go. It would mean putting his career and future on the table, but it was a stake worth making. Win, and it was the big city, with real gun crime, drug dealing gangs and promotion. Failure meant demotion, or worse.

He needed a lot of resources to pull it off, but it was a risk he was happy to take. With his future in his mind's eye full of glory and promise he fired up the Range Rover and headed back to town.

Christie finally fell asleep, still clinging to Tez. In another part of the hospital doctors struggled to revive her dad. He'd had another heart failure, following the damage to his head and chest from the attack. They tried using drugs, not wanting to shock him with broken ribs, but this time it didn't work. The monitor kept it's steady single tone as they worked ventilators, needles and finally the paddles. The senior doctor looked at his colleagues with a small shake of his head as they kept trying to revive the man lying below them, his life slipping away.

Colin, not knowing what was going on, was upbeat as he tinkered with the Skyline, always happy fitting new shiny parts. He had been on an ordering spree, using the cash from the Bull to buy the things he needed to win the grudge match. He had hoped to get the punk kid's car and make it an easy win, but no matter. The car was gone, hidden somewhere he couldn't find, and without the kid, or his bitch to find it. Colin couldn't wait.

He heard a whine of a car stop outside the house and went to see who it was.

"Hey, boss," said Rich, getting out of his Green RX8. "You got that new intake?"

"Yeah," said Colin. "Wanna help?"

"Sure."

They both went into the wooden lean to garage, the Nissan's bonnet was off, resting against the back wall. Two wing protector covers were laid on the sides of the gleaming, shiny engine bay. There wasn't a spot of dirt or oil. Chromed and polished pipes and tubes were neatly routed around the engine, painted the same dark grey of the car. Neon lights were scattered around to light the highly tuned engine bay, but Colin used three large florescent strip lights on the ceiling, and two large workshop lights to make it look like a hospital theatre. He put on a pair of blue latex gloves, and picked the new chromed intake manifold out of the box it came in. Rich looked enviously at it.

"Shiny. You think that will help, boss?" he asked Colin. The smile was all he needed to know. Colin gently placed the manifold on the metal workbench beside the car, and opened another large box. Out came the biggest turbo Rich had ever seen.

"From a truck," Colin explained. "Had a guy in Germany modify it to fit, and do both the manifolds and all the bits."

"Must have cost a bomb," said Rich, looking but not touching the chromed snail.

"Worth it. We can't have those crotch rocket tits clogging the streets any longer." Colin selected a tool from the large sliding chest beside the bench and leant over the engine, the ratchet clicking. Rich stood by, waiting for instructions. Colin called out for spanners, pliers and other tools and Rich passed them to him, feeling like a nurse at an operation. He noted all Colin's tools were in perfect condition, clean and smooth.

After the old manifold was removed, still clean and shiny, Colin fitted the turbo to the new exhaust manifold on the bench.

"So, boss, you got a game plan yet?" asked Rich.

"Why?" said Colin, concentrating.

"Well, I got a grudge with some of them and wanna know where I fit in."

Colin grunted as he tightened bolts. "Not yet, you know that. Gotta meet that dick Mark first and declare who wants to race who."

"Yeah, I guess." Rich tried to sound nonchalant but

Colin put down his tools and looked at him.

"Why the sudden urgency? You knew we have to wait for the official meet."

"Well," said Rich, a little nervously. "You know, just keep getting run ins with those gits and wanna give myself the best chance, that's all."

Colin kept his gaze, making Rich sweat.

"Indeed," said Colin, resuming his work on the manifold. Rich kept quiet as they worked together to slide the big manifold into the crammed engine bay, and fit the new bolts. Colin fitted the leads while Rich did the fuel lines. After two hours Colin dropped into the drivers seat and fired it up. The new turbo whined and hissed, making Colin smile. He fitted the bonnet back on with Rich's help, and smiled at him, conversation forgotten.

"Let's get a beer," he said to Rich when the tools were all cleaned and put away, the car checked and garage tidied.

Rich nodded and followed Colin into the house.

Tez sat on the cold metal chair outside Mary's Café. From here he could see the market square, empty on a Friday, the town hall just after, and the T-junction with the shops at the end, the garage parts shop on the far right. He sipped a more ornate cup of tea in the midday sun, feeling a bit more of a chill as the summer waned. He still wore his bike jacket against the cold, and had his hands around the cup. A few crumbs on a plate was all that remained from his prawn mayo sandwich. He ignored the time, knowing he had a long wait. He had chosen this chair, the only person outside, so he could see, but also be seen. His bike was parked on the other side of the metal rail marking the edge of the café's space. From here he could see everything that came in from the dual-carriage way into the town centre, and into the old area of town with it's small narrow shops and stone built façades. What he waited for he knew would come, and he had to be ready to go.

Sure enough, as the tea grew cold, a dark grey Nissan Skyline warbled past from the dual carriageway. The driver saw the biker watch him go past, and the exhaust note rose as he sped up. Tez drained the cup, vaulted the rail and pulled on his helmet. He thumbed the starter and followed.

The Nissan turned right, heading towards the new shopping centre. Tez followed, not hiding what he was doing. He kept up with the car, indicating when it did, and stopping, or accelerating so he kept the same distance. He saw glimpses through the car's lowered rear window of the driver looking in his centre mirror. With his lights on Tez was easily seen. When the Skyline turned into the shopping centre Tez turned too, but carried on when the car went left into the takeaway car park. As the grey car parked amongst the others outside McDonald's Tez parked his bike on the opposite side of the car park, facing them.

Colin got out the car, looking at the biker. He knew who it was, but why he was being followed troubled him. With his gang around him the kid wouldn't try anything, but what was he doing? The music started, there were only a few cars there, but enough to make it a meet. The kid just sat on his bike, helmet on, engine off. Colin kept up the small talk, mostly about the coming grudge matches, but he kept an eye on the kid.

Ten minutes later the unmistakable rumble of a V8 made everyone look up. The dark shape of Henderson's Range Rover floated past, and parked beside the bike. Nothing was done, the kid still had his helmet on, but they sat together in a near empty car park for a few minutes. Then the bike fired up, raspy high pitched exhaust clear over the thumping bass of the cars' stereos. The biker rode to the group, then past. As he went down the road to the street the kid looked through a tinted visor at the group, then turned left and nailed it, engine howling.

Colin ignored the comments, but was deeply puzzled and feeling worried. Then the big SUV started up and followed the bike. Colin watched it go, face dark with concern.

A short way down the street Tez waited on his bike by the side of the road. He kept the engine running. The Range Rover loomed big in his small mirrors. The car slowed to a stop beside him, and through the windows he saw the inspector nod, then drive off. Tez smiled and headed for home.

19

Saturday morning and old man Hopdyke was surprised to see his best repair man back at work, although not doing any. Instead there was a new car he didn't know up on a ramp. The scattered parts and tools showed the kid had been working for hours.

"Well there. What's all this?" Hopdyke asked.

Tez smiled. "Just doing some long overdue checks and little jobs."

Hopdyke saw the fairly shiny parts in a pile, replaced with brand new ones. Some of the labels he knew, Koni, Willwood, Eibach. Others were new, or not even in English. A stack of stainless tubing was leaning against a wall, the same size as the equally new exhaust pipe fitted to the spotless under body. The wheels, Team Dynamics according to the face, were shod in new low profile tyres, and the open bonnet had pipes hanging out. The smell of oil, weld and petrol was almost overpowering.

"A few checks?" Hopdyke said absently, running a wrinkled finger along a new wishbone on the rear suspension.

"Yeah," said Tez. "Be done in a mo."

Hopdyke looked to the door as the first of the guys turned up for work. He knew they wouldn't be able to resist having a look, and offering advice. Knowing it was a lost cause he left, glad that today looked to be a slow one anyway. Soon there was a crowd around the car, all asking questions or making suggestions. Tez was polite and patient but he knew what he wanted, and two hours later he dropped the bonnet, put the pins in to hold it down, then backed the car gently out, listening for any scraping as the low body crossed the broken concrete and gravel.

On the street he wound up the motor a little, hearing the new exhaust bounce off the shop windows. Heading for the dual carriageway he was soon followed by two marked police cars and the Range Rover. Once on the open road one car headed past, lights and sirens on, the other sat behind with the inspector. Tez slowed to half the speed limit then floored it. The rear of the Volvo kissed the tarmac as it surged forwards. Passing the first patrol car he was clocked at over 140 miles per hour. A police motorbike tried to keep up, but lost him at 170. Stopping at the next junction he turned around and passed them on the way back, going the legal limit. The marked cars turned off their lights and filed in behind Tez. Passing through the town they went south to the airstrip.

Using his map Tez checked the set-up of his car then lined it up on the drag section. An undercover police Mitsubishi Evo sat beside him. Henderson himself waved them off and the Volvo passed the cones at the end five seconds ahead of the police car. The circuit was set out with more cones, and Tez practised it until he could do it blindfolded. Finally the precision driving part. They still didn't know what it involved so Tez mocked up a course to test his abilities both with parking and fast, sharp turns. As the sun began to sink and the fuel light came on Tez stopped and leant on his car, listening to the engine tick itself cool.

"Well?" asked Henderson.

"That'll do it," Tez replied.

Henderson looked dubious. He waved the other cars to go, then leant beside Tez.

"You sure?" he asked the kid.

Tez looked over the airstrip, from the open sided hangers at the end, to the sweeping taxi lane originally laid for the aircraft on the other. The small control tower stood watching by the entrance. Without any other marks to follow Tez felt he had done enough.

"Yeah. I know what I need to change, and how. Just some tweaks and a little fettling."

Henderson stood up and walked to his car. Before getting in he said "just so you know, this goes tits up and your name is on the list too."

Tez smiled and nodded. The big car drove off, leaving him again in silence. He stroked the bonnet, feeling the metal cooling under his hand, the old sponsor stickers starting to fade. It had been a few years since he had raced properly, and a couple since his last street race. Now though he had a reason more then ever to race. Freedom. It wasn't a 'clean your record' storyline. If he won, then he would win everything. Lose, and he loses it all. Not being one to take a risk he had backup plans. Now though, he needed some more practice. Tez got back in, fired it up and headed for fuel, and victims. Tez was back street racing.

Christie was discharged from the hospital the following Monday. Even though Tez was back at work Hopdyke let him pick her up and drop her home. The Black Bull was cold, silent. It had been closed ever since the attack, and the polished bar top was thick with dust. Used pint glasses still lay where the last patrons had left them, on tables, the floor, windowsills. The big windows were shuttered up, forensics dust making paler shades on the counters, door handles and the till. Alvin's jacket was on the back of the chair where he had sat. Christie walked slowly to it, trembling. She reached out to touch it as if it were hot, but stopped just short. Tez put an arm around her, worried her quivering body wasn't ready to come back yet.

He had suggested she stayed at his, but the pub had been empty for a long time, and the police had reported several attempts to break in, prompting them to station a patrol car there most nights. Christie had said she wanted to go home, her home. After all that time in hospital she needed to be on familiar ground. Tez was more concerned Colin would come back to finish what he started.

Christie held him tight, then broke off, heading slowly for the bar. For Tez it felt like being with a close friend on the first visit to a burgled house. Uncomfortable and unsure he followed at a distance, trying to ignore the deserted and unkempt room. Christie passed the bar, and went into the kitchen. Someone had cleaned in here, removing the blood and mess from both the fight and the forensics after. The dark stains on the floor tiles, and the marks on the counter doors still showed signs of the past. Christie put her hand to her mouth and choked back the tears. Tez hovered by the door, letting her have space. She reached out with her other hand and touched the back of a chair by the wooden kitchen table, almost caressing it. She passed around the table, looking first at the edge of the counter by the sink where she had hit her head, then the floor where her father had fallen.

Watching her Tez felt the anger boil again, but held it down. He knew she was hurting, old scars, mental scars reopened. It would be a long time, if ever, when she would recover from those wounds. Satisfied his plan was in motion he waited patiently, not noticing his hand gripped the door knob tight. Christie finished her first lap of the table, stepping around the dark patches on the floor as if her father was still lying there, and went back to where she had been hurt. Looking closely, but not touching the counter edge, she seemed almost childlike in her actions, cocking her head, body bent at near right angles to be as close as possible.

She was still looking when a loud exhaust drove by. Tez tensed briefly, but the car drove past. Christie didn't move. The exhaust note returned, slowed and stopped. Tez let go of the door knob and headed through the bar. Outside he could see the dark grey car of Colin's. Stopping to get the golf club from behind the bar Tez headed out to meet him.

"Whoa!" yelled Colin seeing Tez emerge from the dark pub with the club raised over his head.

"Whoa yourself. You think you can come here? Ain't you done enough?" Tez kept the club high, like a baseball player.

"I heard she was out, just wanted to see she was ok,"

Colin said, hands held out in front of himself.

"Yeah, she's ok, no thanks to you," said Tez.

Colin looked puzzled. "Thanks to me?"

Tez gave him credit. He was a good actor. "I know who did it, you bastard," he said softly. "You ever step foot in here again you'll leave the same way Alvin did, if you're bloody lucky."

Colin waved his hands, but backed away slowly. "Look, Kid. I have no idea who did this. I've been looking myself. You gotta believe me." He dropped his arms. "Well, if she's ok that's all I need to know. Tell her if she needs anything she only has to ask."

"How about your balls on a silver platter?" Tez said, club still raised.

Colin smiled. It wasn't a smile of a nice person. Tez struggled not to shiver. That was the smile from a horror film. Colin got back into his car, but kept eye contact, not looking scared, more smug. He drove off, spraying gravel over the front of the pub as he left.

Inside Christie was still staring at the corner, one hand reaching out but not touching it. Tez leant on the door frame to the kitchen, wiping sweat from his face. He still held the club. Christie looked up, didn't say anything but saw the club, and went out to the stairs.

In her room everything was still there, just dusty. Tez opened the window to freshen the air while Christie shamelessly stripped naked. Wrapped in a silk robe she went for a shower, Tez noticed the thin patch on her head from the attack. With little to do Tez went back downstairs to bolt the front door, then waited in the kitchen. Poking around the cupboards he found plenty of out of date food, a fridge that almost held it's own ecosystem, and bread that could nearly walk. Taking a black bin bag he cleared everything out, using hot water

to wipe clean every cupboard, surface and door. Then he got a mop and bucket, with plenty of detergent, and cleaned the kitchen floor, heading into the dark bar. Without realising the time he spent two hours cleaning, wiping, polishing and washing until the bar looked like it used to, the kitchen was bare, but clean, and the windows let in the afternoon light when he opened the shutters. The back door to the yard showed marks from attempted break ins, but still locked so he went around checking every lock and bolt to be sure. When Christie emerged from the bathroom, having showered and soaked in the bath the pub looked almost back to normal.
The smell of a Chinese take away tempted her downstairs. Wrapped in a large fluffy towel, another on her hair like a snail shell, she smiled thankfully and ate.

"Think we need to do a spot of shopping," Tez said, piling into his chow mien.

Christie nodded. After her shower she looked like she used to, just the bags of worry under her eyes. Tez reached out and held her hand. They shared a moment, eyes locked, her hand gripped tighter.

"I best get myself sorted," she said, between mouthfuls. "Can't go out in a towel."

"Why not," said Tez. "The Romans did."

"Yeah, but they had warmer weather." Christie laughed, the sound welcome in the silence. They finished their food,
Tez picking on the prawn crackers while she went upstairs. An hour, and a whole bag of crackers later, she came down in her old clothes, denim skirt, short top, laden with jewellery and make up. Tez felt the warmth stir inside him. It was what she wore when they first met. She was starting over again.

Christie got the big bunch of keys and waited for him to

go before locking every door. In her car they drove to the supermarket, holding hands, smiling.

20

At the garage on Tuesday morning Tez dived into his work with gusto. The fears of the past, his past and others, were lifted. He had everything set in place, and enough time to do a few more speed checks and test runs on the track. The guys at the garage, more impressed and respectful then ever, now treated him like a celebrity, a man they all admired, wanted to be. Old Hopdyke was happy his star worker was back, and with the late summer came a lot of business as people parked their cars for the winter and wanted them checking and sorting.

By lunch Tez was back at the sandwich bar next to the shop, this time surrounded by his co-workers. They laughed, joked and insulted each other over bacon, sausage and egg meals, mass made tea and plenty of camaraderie. Tez felt accepted, as if he had passed some initiation test and become part of an elite group, a fully paid up member. The thought of leaving that had plagued him before was a distant memory, smothered by the good feeling of the present. Christie had kept him warm last night, making him sweat in her small bed, lying on top of the blankets as they panted naked together.

Cars drove by the large glass window overlooking the street and market square. Every car that was modified was graded by the group, with passing jeers and comments on each other's scoring. The staff watched and joined in, the good feeling flowing like energy, magnetising everyone towards itself. A few bikes rode past, getting some attention, but not much. Tez absently thought about his bike, and if he should sell it, or just get a better one. The meal passed far too fast, and they shuffled back to work, still bickering in the way only happy and relaxed men can do with those they trust.

Back in the yard Tez saw the pink car, Christine's car. Heading into the office he saw her chatting to one of the girls. As usual the sight of her tanned legs under a short skirt, tanned belly under a shorter top, and shapely chest all on show made him stop, swallow, and hope his jeans were loose enough not to show his reaction. She smiled, making it worse, and left the shop girl, stepping gracefully in very high heels, and kissed him, raising one leg like they do in the movies. She giggled at his reaction, still staring dumbly at her. It was the first time really since before she was attacked he had seen her fully made up. Hair styled in long blonde spiral curls that hung down her smooth face, tanned, with full celebrity make up she looked like a glamour model. She squeezed both his hands and kissed him again, more tenderly, more passionately.

"Hey, err, hey," Tez managed.

"Hey you too," she smiled. "You coming over later?"

"Yeah, of course," said Tez, feeling silly in front of the shop girls.

"You better," she said, punching him playfully on the chest. "Gonna cook you something special." She moved closer, speaking sexily. "And if you like the food, you'll love the cook, especially the way I cook." She smiled in a flirty, dirty way, and stepped back. The shop girls heard it all, and were almost envious of the blonde girl.

A cough made them both look. Hopdyke looked disapprovingly from under his bushy grey eyebrows, like a grumpy owl.

"Got work, kid?" he asked.

Tez was about to speak when Christie stepped towards the old man, head down, walking one foot over the other, until she got close. Then she looked into his eyes, bent slightly forwards so he could see down her top.

"Sure my man works hard enough to earn a little time with his girl?" she asked, so softly and sexually even Hopdyke blushed.

"Whatever," he said, uncomfortable, and left.

Christie walked back, full of confidence Tez hadn't seen in ages, and sorely missed.

"Be there half six, stud," she said as she passed him, still walking. "Don't be late."

They all watched her hips wiggle out, the girls spitting silent venom, Tez feeling the need for a quick toilet break.

In the yard three customer's cars waited to be seen to, one awaited collection, and two were staff cars owned by the mechanics. Nobody really paid much attention to the old battered Toyota Avensis that coasted into a space, or the man who got out and walked away, past the garage office, and around the corner into the street. The blokes were back at work, cars on ramps, radio loud tuned to a local radio station. There was nothing unusual, or even strange until the phone rang. Hopdyke answered it before the shop girls, who were still discussing how slutty the blonde looked.

"Hopdyke Garage," he said gruffly.

"You don't know me," said an electronic voice, "but I have a message for you. We don't like troublemakers here, and those who keep them are equal. Good bye."

The line went dead.

Hopdyke looked at the handset, then put it back down. He'd had some strange calls in the past, some insinuating Hopdyke was a criminal, some threatening violence. This, like the others he ignored.

One of the mechanics finished his jobs, and having added his customers car to the line up he spotted the

Toyota. A bit confused why it was there he asked in the office, but they hadn't heard about it. Hopdyke, forgetting the phone call, told him to check inside if it was unlocked, and if the keys were in, to move it out the way. The mechanic checked for anything in the glove box, and finding nothing decided to move the car, that was part blocking the yard exit.

The sound of the car exploding was silent. Everyone said they heard nothing. The fireball that filled the yard and mushroomed over the rooftops did make a sound, like a gas lantern being lit. Windows blew out, the office rocked so violently cracks formed in the old brickwork. Stock fell off shelves, those close by had to steady themselves. Hopdyke was knocked to the floor as he tried to sit. Tez, in the small painted brick toilet cubicle, was thrown against the wall, hitting his head hard and leaving a red smear. Everyone behind a wall was dazed and bruised, but guys in the garage stood no chance. With the open doors the blast swept them all aside, smashing bodies and equipment. One car was launched from the ramp it was on through the wall and into the kitchen of the house built behind, passing though the small alley that separated them.

In the police station Henderson put down the phone in his tiny office, worried. People didn't make prank calls to his direct line, and with a digital voice changer, without being serious. The threat had been against him, and what the caller referred to as his accomplices. Thinking fast he knew they were talking about the kid and his plan to stop the gangs. He had always pegged Colin as being the violent type, his attack on the girl was proof enough.

Looking out the small window, first to his car sat sleeping by the curb, then over the town, his mind raced. The floor vibrated, a rumble like the earthquake he'd felt in Malta years ago. He knew that feeling all too well. As his door flew open it let the shocked face of a constable in. Henderson was on the way out, leaving the man explain to an empty room.

The police arrived first, as you would expect, their station being yards down the road. The ambulances and fire engines were only minutes behind, coming from their stations straddling the dual carriageway. Henderson was in the thick of things, smoke and dust surrounding him like a medieval monster. Covered in soot his smart suit was smudged and creased as he sweated his way through the near extinguished, and near demolished garage. Firstly, on coming into the yard on foot he saw the twisted remains of a bombed car in the middle of the yard, the roof peeled open like a flower. Then he saw the smoke billow from the open garage. He ignored the screams from in the office. Screaming meant alive. Henderson ran into the smoke, realising it wasn't from a fire, but the blast, trapped in the open mouth of the garage bays. He saw through streaming eyes the scorched and surprised bodies of the mechanics, some still holding tools. Most were hairless, some stripped of their clothes too. It reminded him of the blast at Pompeii, a place he'd once visited.

He hurriedly got on with the grim task of checking the bodies, all dead. The kid wasn't there. In the remains of the paint booth Henderson saw the kid's bike, saved from the blast by the edge of the wall. It was on it's side having been pushed against the booth door, but intact. Still short of a body Henderson ran into the shop, muscling the door open, the wall was actually bowed inwards, the door frame out of true. Inside there was clouds of dust and patchy light from holes in the old ceiling. In the shop itself the plate windows out front were whole, but cracked. Parts and things from the shelves lay scattered on the floor, one of the cute girls from the shop was crying, holding her bleeding leg. The other was trying to open a green first aid kit. Henderson passed them, ignoring the pleading look from the struggling girl, and went through the store room and into the back office. He found old Hopdyke trying to stand. He'd been heading back into his office when the car blew. His back wall, his office being beside the reception, was also bent inwards like a big water balloon.

Henderson helped the old man up, noting the small line of blood on his forehead. Once the man was back in his chair Henderson leant on the dusty desk as if conducting an interview with a criminal.

"Where's the kid?" he asked the old man.

Hopdyke looked under his eyebrows, made bigger by the dust. He looked confused, lost, the face of an old man with a child's fear.

Henderson resisted the urge to slap him. Instead he took a breath, leant close and asked again. The old man shook his head. Henderson grunted and left, slamming the door. The sound of something falling made him nearly smile. He went out the front to the café to see if the kid was in there, and finding it empty he headed back to the garage. Sirens and lights announced the rest of the emergency services.

Pushing the task of incident control onto someone else Henderson went back into the garage to search.

The back wall was out, a gaping hole where a car had been pushed through. Poking his head through Henderson saw the alley was empty. Feeling a little desperate amidst all the chaos he nearly called out, then went back to the yard. He choked back tears of relief when he saw the kid stagger out the back door, reeling like a drunk. A paramedic caught him, and helped him sit down.

Tez winced as the medic pressed a white bandage to his head, feeling more like it was a brick at speed. He felt dizzy and sick, not a good sign. Confused he tried to figure out what was going on, and gave up. His eyes weren't focusing properly, so he closed them. The paramedic was speaking to him, but Tez didn't care much to talk.

"Hey, kid," said another voice.

Forcing his eyes open, feeling more pain as the light flooded in, Tez saw a fuzzy figure looking down.

"Come on, kid. I'll get you checked out." The voice held out a shape towards Tez, and the shape gripped his arm and lifted him up. The world swam slightly, making him wonder if he'd been drinking. Not that you tend to get the hangover when drunk, but you never know.

The voice led him away like a wounded soldier from battle. In the soft confines of a car Tez slowly realised where he was. The rumble of a big V8 up front, and the big soft armchair brought him around.

"Henderson?" he asked in a tiny voice.

"Yeah, kid. You ok?"

Tez shook his head, and wished he hadn't. Holding onto the door handle he took a few deep breaths and tried again.

"Not really. What happened?"

"Your mate, Colin," said Henderson, driving.

"Colin?"

"Yeah. Think he wants you out the way. Not seen him go this far, but he can only get you here, or at home."

Tez tensed up so violently Henderson thought he was having a heart attack. His dirty face looked fearsome with wide, wet eyes floating in the middle.

"Home!" he shouted. "Home! Must go home. Christie."

Henderson cursed under his breath and swung the big car around. He flipped an unmarked switch and a siren wailed, small lights in the corners of the windscreen flashing blue. Swerving hard he dived through the traffic, past red lights and speed bumps, the air suspension soaking up the punishment as he drove south. Tez leant forwards, looking through the big windscreen for any sign of smoke ahead. They both let out a sigh when they saw the Black Bull standing intact and almost asleep. The windows were shuttered up, doors closed. Upstairs a curtain was pulled aside and Christie looked out at the SUV that slid on the gravel outside. Seeing Tez in the passenger seat, bandage to his head, she ran downstairs and out to meet them. Henderson grabbed her arm and threw her into the back seat.

"What the hell?" she started, but Henderson was already going, gravel spraying from all four wheels as he drifted the car around and out onto the road. Christine was about to speak when the car rocked, as if by a sudden wind. Behind them the windows of the Bull blew out into the car park. Black smoke billowed from the twisted shutters. Upstairs the windows shattered, curtains flicking out the frames. The chimney puffed a stream of sooty smoke, the chimney pot launching into the air. Henderson pulled to the side of the road and they all watched.

When the dust settled the pub looked almost undamaged, save the broken windows and dust clouds lazily drifting out.

Christine had her hand over her mouth, and looked to Henderson, as did Tez.

"Gas," said the inspector. "I smelt something when we pulled in, and when she came down I realised they must have opened a pipe inside, under the bar. Surprised you didn't smell it," he said to Christine.

"I didn't notice," she said, apologetically. "Lost most of my sense of smell, and I was worried about Tez. You ok, babe?"

Tez nodded, and winced. "We can't go back to mine. Probably be a crater by now."

Henderson agreed. "I think now you are both under police protection. I know a place. We can get you some new clothes on the way."

As he turned the car around and headed past the Bull Christie still covered her mouth, and silent tears fell. Tez watched the pub pass blankly. He tapped the inspector's hand gently.

"We need to make a stop, first," Tez said, watching the road ahead.

"What for?" asked Henderson.

"Need to check on something," replied Tez, who refused to answer any more questions and sat in brooding silence, only calling lefts and rights as the inspector drove. Christie sat in the back, unsure what was going on, but longing for the happiness she had lost since summer began. Maybe not happiness but she had lost something inside. Her youth maybe?

As the car headed down Tez's mystery tour all three had plenty to think about.

21

The old farmer looked happily at Tez, amused at Christie and open loathing to Henderson. He openly took in the lithe figure of Christine, making them wait, then slapped Tez on the back so hard he nearly fell over.

"So, young 'un, what you after?" he said in a gruff but friendly voice.

"Need a place to lay low," replied Tez, rubbing his shoulder.

The farmer laughed, and offered a coarse work hardened hand to Christie, who took it as if it were poisoned. This made the man laugh even more.

"Pleasure, young lady. Welcome to my little patch of land.
Name's Phipps."

"Christie," she murmured, moving closer to Tez.

"My casa is your casa," he said. "All are welcome." He smiled to the young couple then turned to Henderson, the smile dropping like a shot bird. "But not you. No pigs on my farm."

Henderson shrugged, got back into his car and drove away. When he had gone Phipps giggled and turned back to Tez.

"So, young 'un, I bet you wanna check your little toy, eh?"

Tez nodded, and they led Christie around the back of the old stone farmhouse, past some metal roofed sheds filled with cows and smells, and almost out the farmyard, stopping at a half brick, half metal shed. Phipps paused, almost uncertain, but held his smile. To Christie he seemed like a loveable old uncle, without his own kids, so enjoying any time with anyone else's.

"Now then, young Missy," he said. "This 'ere is my private place. My inner sanctum I guess you could call it." He adjusted his flat cap absently as he spoke. "Never showed anyone, even the wife, God rest her soul. Only the kid here, after all he did for me."

He shot Tez a fatherly smile, making him actually blush

slightly.

"Anyway," Phipps continued still fingering the key chain in one hand. "In 'ere is my little treasure chest. Some have been out before, some not, but never recently. Please be a bit careful," he finished, unlocking the door.

As he swung it open the first thing she noticed was how thick it was. The smell of engine oil, petrol and polish wafted out to the cooling afternoon air. Phipps went inside and flicked on the lights. Unlike the other farm shed, all stained concrete and leaking tin roofs, this one was spotless. The floor was painted in red garage floor paint, the walls an off white so the florescent strip lights bounced the shadows away. Lined up in two rows were five cars under soft cotton covers. Phipps still stood by the door, hand on the light switch. He cast his eyes over his collection lovingly, a father with five well loved children.

Tex passed him and went to the first car. Sliding the cover off Christie saw it was his Volvo, spotless and gleaming. Phipps seemed to want to compete, taking the covers off the others slowly, like a reveal at a car launch. The line up was staggering.

There stood a 1964 Pontiac GTO, an E-Type Jaguar, a 1969 Mustang, something she couldn't recognise but looked futuristic in a historical sort of way, and the last was a dark blue Dodge Charger, the intake and supercharger sticking up through the wide, flat bonnet like a chrome iceberg. This last car Phipps ran a loving, but gentle, hand over, from the broad boot, over the sweeping shoulder and stopping on the roof by the door.

"They didn't make a decent one after 1970," he said. Christie looked shocked but in a good way, resisting the urge to touch the exotic cars. Tez finished checking the Volvo, and helped Phipps put the covers back on. With the light off, and an alarm set they headed for the house.

In the large, and ageing front room Phipps gave them both a mug of tea in stained beakers, dropping into a sagging wing back arm chair as they sat on the equally decrepit settee. After a long sip on his tea Phipps let out a sigh.

"Guess you're wonderin' where all that came from, eh Missy?" he said. Christie nodded, cradling her tea in both hands. The house was cold, no central heating. But a large fire in the hearth made it almost too warm, the smell of smoke, and the crackle of wood seemed soothing and calming. Tez felt as safe as he could be, listening to the old man speak, Christie's leg touching his.

"Well," started Phipps, settling into his chair. "See, thing is, back in the war my folks were either fighting the Hun over there, or fighting for the home back here. I was just a bit young to be in it, but I joined at the end. Just in time for the victory parades," he laughed, a dry rattle making them a bit worried for his health. "Anyway, me dad came home one day, after old Adolph quit, with a Yank in tow. He was a good laugh, bit older than me. He had some funny ass stories I can tell you. We got on well enough, even visited his place in Wisconsin. He started trying to get us to move over, but me old lady, God rest her soul, didn't like the life over there. We talked about it, but never did go. I took a fancy to a big old car, a Cadillac it was. Big as a bus and twice as thirsty. I joked with old Bill about getting one over here, but knew it would never happen. Two months after we got home he turns up on me doorstep waving some keys. Turns out he got himself an old transport boat cheap and shipped the damned car over 'ere."

Phipps paused to drink some of his tea. He noticed his audience were enthralled in his story, so decided to spin it out a bit.

"So there was I with a flaming great Cadillac El' Dorado, in grey an' all. No idea what to do with the bloody thing, pardon my language, missy. We asked around, got it registered and all road legal, like. The looks when it drove into town!" He leant back and barked a laugh. "Course the town were a lot smaller in them days. Better too wi'out that stupid shopping bit and the new build boxes they all go nuts for. That Caddy got some serious looks. This were the sixties after all, and that car were only a couple of year old. Turns out Bill had made some cash flogging old kit and got himself a business shipping stuff over the pond. He asked me to join, and with me discharge cash burning a hole in me pocket I jumped at the chance. Soon I were on his boat helping to get cars over 'ere."

He drained his cup, and looked sadly into the beige depths. Christie stood without a word and took the cup, headed for the kitchen. Both men watched her leave, and return with a steaming cup. Phipps took a sip, eyes widening.

"Bloody hell, missy! Best cup I 'ad in years. You can stay long as you like." Phipps took another sip as Christie blushed. He set the cup down on the ring marked coffee table and resumed his tale.

"By the seventies we had a lot of cash knocking around, but me dad were ill with pneumonia. Mum wanted me to take over the family farm, so I did. Kept up with Bill of course, but the money stopped. Then he asked if he could keep some 'ere until he sold 'em. I were happy with that. He paid me in cars so that suited. The Dodge were me best choice. Tax free and made by me and Bill. Used to have a paint booth, ramps, our own little garage. Ship them 'ere, strip and rebuild, then sell for a bomb. Then

Bill got sick himself. He didn't last a month. All that sea air I thinks. So it all stopped. Bugger still owed me half a car, but I'll let 'im off that." Phipps took another sip, settling back with a groan of satisfaction.

"I was gonna give up on 'em, sell 'em, but I met this kid 'ere and he helped get them running. Told him to take the Mustang as payment, but he won't. Good kid, bit soft, but good." Phipps nodded to Tez, who leant back and looked to the ceiling. He knew some of this, but the old man was in full swing and nothing would stop him now.

"So when Tez needed a place for his car," Christie said.

"I let 'im. Why not? He's helped me a lot, least I could do." Phipps leant forwards with a conspirational wink. "And having him 'ere means I get more done," he said softly.

Christie laughed and the old man leant back in his chair.

"Proper cuppa, missy." he said, draining the cup again. "You kids get the back room. Overlooks the sheds. Nice view when the sun sets for you. Go to bed now. Let an old man sit in peace."

They thanked him and left, arm in arm. He watched them, especially the girls long legs, with a phantom smile. Leaving the television off he looked out the window at the drive to the road. He was in his home, his castle. It was safe, but soon the enemy would be invading his castle. He would be ready.

22

Colin sat at the park bench over looking the town. The sun was gone now, the autumn settling in for the season. Below him, past patchwork fields of greens, browns and yellows, the town slept under the late evening sky. Colin was irritated, as usual, but this time it was more than just other people getting on his nerves. That damn kid had escaped with the pub whore, and now Colin just knew the bastard would step up. The copper must be tapping the kid, making the dumb bugger do his dirty work. Colin knew Henderson was a sly one. Before Colin had kicked out a member for being a snitch, and he knew there was another.

He waited for the right time to pounce, but the mole could wait before he got his due. Now it was business.

  Checking the Seiko watch on his wrist Colin grunted and stood. Behind him most of his group were in the small gravel car park. The cars shone in the dull light. The girls defied the cold in their skimpy clothes, the guys in open hoodies and some still in sleeveless shirts. Eyeing his troops Colin made a mental note of who to speak to about their cars, and who he was going to pummel into a burger for being the grass. Satisfied they all seemed presentable, checking the girls closely, Colin waved a hand in the air, then got into his Skyline. The others followed suit and with the roar of a fleet of loud performance exhausts Colin led them out the car park and down the road. It was time.

  Mark shook his head sadly, the smile he always wore was gone today. The sound of the cars grew louder. Sat on the cold concrete runway Mark had lined up his guys like soldiers in Wellington's army, waiting for the enemy. He looked to the gateway, ponytail whipping his cheek. The creak of leathers, the squeak of biker boots, and held breath mixed with the exhaust noise.

  Colin led the line up into the airfield, parking in the middle so he faced his brother's bike. The rest lined up on both sides. Colin got out and walked, head down, to his brother, who tried to smile.

"So, your pussies ready?" asked Colin with venom.

The smile slipped into a crooked grimace. "Yeah, we are. You?" replied Mark.

"Ready to hand your ass to you, twat," he spat.

Mark shook his head, and looked into the hate filled eyes of his blood brother.

"Col, seriously," he began, but was cut off.

"Nobody calls me that!" Colin near screamed. "Nobody! You watch that tongue of yours or I will pull it out through your arse you gimp dressed freak."

Mark was taken aback, lost for words. His face went red, but he held out his hands to stop anyone stepping up to retaliate.

"Ok, Colin," he said eventually. "If you really want to do this."

Colin smiled an evil smile that chilled Mark's heart, turned and strode off. He stopped by his car, still facing away. He turned back slowly, arms out like a bank robber giving in to the police.

"So," Colin called loudly enough to be heard by everyone. "This is grudge time. Anyone has anything they want to settle, any score to even, here is your chance. Call them out." He leant on his car as one by one eight of his guys stood up and called the names. After a long pause Colin stood.

"I call that bit of shit there," he said, pointing to Mark.

Before Mark could respond the noise of both four and eight cylinder cars were heard getting close fast. All looked to the gateway and in flew a red Corsa, black Range Rover, and shiny silver Volvo. The Corsa peeled to the left, Range Rover to the right, letting the Volvo come between so they stopped at the end of the line together. Tez got out first, followed by Christie in clothes to rival the 4power girls.

Henderson got out slower, with menace.

"I call out Mark, and Colin Hopwood," said Tez. He looked down both lines, feeling the warmth of his girl on his right arm.

Mark smiled, amused. Colin seemed ready to explode.

"You what?" Colin asked, dark and menacing.

"I call you and your brother," replied Tez.

At the word 'brother' Colin visibly jumped as if someone had walked over his grave. His face contorted into such rage Tez took a step back. Colin walked down the line at speed, his brother following with a more ambling gait.

"You call me?" asked Colin, his face in Tez's.

"Yeah," replied Tez, not backing down.

"You got something worth betting?"

Tez smiled and patted the bonnet of his car. "Yeah. Everything."

Colin gave a half grin. "Everything?

"Everything." Tez was firm in his voice, but the eyes showed fear.

"You know everything includes your car?" Colin said, almost friendly.

"Naturally," said Tez.

"And your home, and money?"

"Yeah."

Colin leant closer, voice still kept high and clear. "And your woman?"

Tez hesitated. Colin sensed the worry and spoke softly.

"Just walk away, little boy. Leave your car, take your slut, and walk. Only way. If you don't, then you walk out of town butt naked, and with only the knowledge your bitch will be crying and bleeding when my guys have had their fun."

Tez tensed, but held himself back.

"Everything," he said loudly, still staring defiantly at Colin.

"I accept," said Mark, leaning on the Corsa. Colin shot him a look of pure irritation. He knew he couldn't back down.

"And so do I," Colin said through forced teeth. "But we combine the races. We do the precision and the circuit together."

"Good," agreed Tez. He waited until Colin backed off, then got back into his car. Henderson and Christie did the same and the trio left the two gangs to finalise their races, and wagers.

In the empty car park of the Bull Tez pulled over. He got out and bent over, trying not to be sick. Christie stopped behind him, and held him as best she could, feeling the tremble in his body. Henderson pulled up alongside, window rolled down.

"Well done, kiddo," he said to Tez's back. "You gonna do fine."

Tez turned his head and smiled weakly. Christie gave an annoyed look, and tried to help him stand up. Henderson left them alone, he had work to do. Getting a drink from the closed and boarded up pub Christie made sure Tez was better, then let him follow her back to the farm.

Phipps was waiting with his usual beaming smile, and open arms.

"Hey there, young 'un. You looks a bit peaky. Best be getting inside. I'll lock your car up. Got a plate of hot stew on the Aga, and some cider in the pantry. Thinks you need a nip or three."

Tez thanked the old man and went up the step to the house, Christie still holding him. Phipps watched her walk in, half bent over, in case of a flash of panty, then drove the cars around the back. Being the man he was he washed them both, letting them drip dry outside, then driving them into the shed, where under the lights he polished them both, admiring and checking the bodywork as he did.

Inside, Tez had his third helping of stew and belched loudly. Christie looked shocked and slapped him on the back of the head with a tea towel. Tez just laughed.

"You really think you can win?" she asked while he spooned stew into his mouth hungrily. Tez rather liked the old man's cooking, the coal fired Aga made it taste better somehow.

Tez nodded, swallowed and grinned. "Beat anything on the road, that thing of mine. Don't forget I won every class when I did track racing. Plus I tested and set up the car on their course before I called them out."

Christine nodded, but still looked uncertain. Tez put down his spoon and laid his hand on hers.

"Don't panic. I got a plan," he said, giving her hand a squeeze. She smiled back and went to do the dishes. Tez watched her, worried. Normally she was cheerful doing chores. Tez often joked she was the only person in the world enjoyed cleaning. Today she worked in silence, dunking plates and glasses in the stone sink without even a trace of a smile. Tez finished his stew, wiped the plate with a chunk of bread, and took it to the sink. Christie thanked him quietly, and washed it. Tez waited, looking at her back, then left to check on the car.

"You sure?" asked Colin. They stood in the driveway of Colin's house, away from the noise of the party inside.

"Yeah," said Martin. "Followed them there."

Colin smiled, then laughed, slapping Martin on the back.

"Perfect. That old fart's been lazy. Think we may have a surprise visit next week. That little whore of his will make a nice toy for the games room, don't you think?"

Martin nodded, but hid his fear. Colin had become more and more erratic of late. The bombings were a sign he was going too far. Martin knew not to question Colin, he had known him since first school. But sometimes Colin did get carried away.

Martin took the beer offered, even though his thirst had gone. Around them the post call out party was in full swing. Three girls were having a kissing contest with each other, two girls were topless, dancing to the drunken cheers of the watching guys. Some were already going upstairs, the spare room already having a small queue forming. Martin drained his bottle and wondered, not for the first time, if he really wanted to be here, then saw one of the trio of girls was stripping another, got a second beer and sat down to watch.

23

Phipps had become a bit of a prowler of late. He knew how to stalk prey, hunt animals, and even people. Owning a farm in England through the eighties gave him a special skill at both offensive and defensive stalking. Now he checked his small arsenal comprising of his only legal weapon, a side by side 12 gauge shotgun, two mildly illegal sub machine guns from his shipping days, and a very illegal revolver from America, chromed and garish. He had bought it from a gun shop in New Orleans once, liking the Dirty Harry look, and never used it. Stashing it in his kit on the boat it never saw the sea air so kept the smooth polished finish. Even now it stayed in the metal gun cabinet, wrapped in velvet, sleeping. Beside the cabinet were a few extra supplies he had stashed. Four flack jackets from the war, a bullet proof vest he'd swiped from a police van in the nineties, a tear gas launcher, without canisters, and some camouflage gear. He never thought he'd need it, but being a bit of a hoarder Phipps had kept it all, and maintained it, just in case.

Now the old man adjusted his cap and caressed the shotgun gently with one finger. The old, scratched barrel was marked from years of abuse, but inside it was spotless, oiled and ready. Phipps loaded two shells, checking inside the barrel for muck first, and dropped the remaining rounds into his jacket pocket. As an afterthought he slung one of the machine guns over his shoulder. Locking the gun room door he turned off all the lights in the house, waited for ten minutes, and sneaked outside.

In the cool evening air the summer seemed long gone. Leaves were beginning to brown and the air was sharp. Phipps saw his breath cloud before his face, so he breathed out the side of his mouth. Keeping low he left the back door, following the brick wall that lined the kitchen garden, and watched from the corner. The yard was silent. All the cattle were out in the fields, the weather being warm enough, for now. Distant cars passed, normal, quiet cars. Knowing if anything was going to happen it would be fast and sudden Phipps tensed his ageing frame and scuttled to the shed. Checking the doors and alarm he settled in an old wood pile he'd made. The pile covered a small shed which had a comfy chair, heater and no light. Inside he could see all, but not be seen. Prepared for a long night Phipps hung the smaller gun on a bit of wood, laid the shotgun on his lap, and waited.

Henderson also burned the midnight oil. The reports from the car bomb slowly filtered in. The car was stolen from over town, plates changed, and filled with a mix of diesel, petrol and mining explosives, also stolen from a nearby quarry. CCTV showed the driver dump the car, but hide his face. It looked like Tiny, one of Colin's guys, but the image was too poor to prove it. Henderson often cursed CCTV for being so useless. You could see the crime, but not the criminal. Why bother?

The bomb was on a timer, Henderson found in the initial report. Probably set to the time the kid came back from lunch. Lucky he needed a crap or he would be gone too. The garage was written off, major structural damage. Would more than likely be pulled down and rebuilt. The grieving relatives tried to come to terms with the loss, and the town mayor had been over, insisting on a swift resolution to the crime. Henderson told the surprised man that he knew who had done it, and was gathering evidence already. This settled the mayor, and probably the families when they were told the same. Henderson promised himself the perpetrators would pay for it.

Putting the report down Henderson picked up the cheap office phone, dialled an outside number and waited impatiently. Finally there was an answer.

"Yellow," said the phone.

"Henderson, Lower Hampton police."

"Ah, yes. Still going on with your plan?"

Henderson nodded, even though the man on the phone couldn't see. "Yeah, I am. Can you meet?"

"Sure," said the phone. "Got something new?"

"Nope. Just want to be sure we all know what's going on."

"You asked for my help, Henderson. I won't screw up my side."

"I know." Henderson smiled at his own cunning. "You got it?"

"I planned it," said the phone. "Now bugger off. Security and all."

The phone went dead. Henderson put the receiver down and leant back. Things were looking up. The grudge matches were a week away, everything was sorted, the kid was in hiding somewhere with his wonder car. Hopwood was lining up for his jail sentence, and after the bomb Henderson would be recognised, maybe nationally, as the man who wiped out a whole gang war in one fell swoop. Yeah, things were looking up. Henderson decided to treat himself to a kebab from the chip shop on the way home, even though it stank the car out. Who cares? Time to celebrate.

Tez rolled over in the ridiculously comfortable bed, feeling Christie moan in her sleep at being disturbed. He felt bad, but he had to lie to the old man. Safety. He couldn't lose. With the curtains closed the room was black, but in the darkness his eyes adjusted and the shadowy shape of the bed, chest of drawers and wardrobe slowly formed. He saw the pale blur of Christie's face on her pillow, and tried to make out the details. He couldn't fail her.

Sitting in bed, feeling the cold on his bare back, Tez looked at her and felt fear. If he lost, or something happened he didn't doubt Colin would make her his whore, using her body whenever he wanted, or didn't want, just to get back at Tez. The thought of her soft skin under Colin's harsh grip made Tez tremble with anger, shoulders tensed. Forcing himself to calm Tez knew he was a prepared as he could be. He knew the ability of Colin's car, and his own. He knew he could win, should win. But as every real racer knows there is no easy victory.

Tez slid off the bed and walked naked to the soft armchair, one of many spread around the old farm house.

Even in the cold, with no central heating, he sat crossed legged, looking at Christie's sleeping form. He couldn't sleep, as much as he wanted to. He couldn't fail her. He will not fail her.

24

It was well past midnight, the autumn chill making his old bones ache. Phipps sat huddled in a thick old blanket in his wood pile shelter. Large black gloves covered cold fingers, wrapped around the old shotgun. He was starting to doze, the hip flask nearly empty of it's warming liquor. He suddenly snapped wide awake, the instinctive reaction of an old soldier. He didn't see anyone, but he sensed them. Silently he unwrapped the blanket, hoping it was another fox. It wasn't.

The half stooped man ran briefly from one patch of dark to another. Phipps almost laughed. He looked like one of those stupid video games the kids played, soldiers in a future world running around, coming back after they died to fight again. This kid was trying to look professional, and by the stocky shape following him Phipps could see why. He didn't go into town much, but he knew old man Hopwood well, and he knew his kids, as everyone did. Colin moved with purpose, slapping the first kid for his stupidity, and crossed the yard brazenly in the security lights. He wore a balaclava and padded black jacket, but there was no hiding his bulk, that muscular shape underneath.

As expected they went straight for the cars. Phipps thought he would break in and try to sabotage the kid's car, but when the man stopped and waved to the others

Phipps paused, waiting. Three more ran up, looking like henchmen from the old Batman series in the '60's. Two carried big plastic tubs. They looked heavy. Phipps had seen enough. He checked the breach of his shotgun and stood. As he went to leave his little shelter the sound of breathing behind him stopped him. He had been a fool, and he realised it now. Something hard pressed into his back. He didn't need to look to see it was a knife. Dropping his head Phipps lowered the shotgun. The knife moved away. Phipps was about to turn when fireworks exploded in his head, and the world blissfully went dark.

Colin moved his men fast, pushing and slapping them. It was taking too long. Five more came from around the shed, all with empty tubs. About fifty gallons of petrol had been poured around the garage. With a smile Colin flicked a lit match into the pool. To ruin the effect it went out before it landed. Muttering a curse he lit three at once, and dropped them on the edge of the damp earth. The fuel caught instantly and the flames roared around the shed, hiding it in black smoke. With a nod of satisfaction Colin turned and ran. Some paused to watch the rising inferno, but soon all eight were sprinting after him.

Tez saw the glow through the bedroom window, and almost tore the thin curtains away. The shed was now well up, the slowly moving form of Phipps on the floor nearby. Tex threw on jeans and a shirt, and ran downstairs. Christie called after him, but he ignored her. Once in the yard he ran barefooted over the old cobbles and mud to Phipps. The old man had an impressive gash to his head, and was a bit groggy, but he could stand and with the help of Tez watched the shed collapse.

"Sorry, young 'un. Guess I'm too old for this crap," he

said, eyes reflecting the flames.

"Don't worry about it," said Tez, steering the old man away and back to the house.

Inside Christie was wearing his t shirt, which was a little too short, showing her black panties. Phipps saw straight away, stopping and smiling the grin of a dirty old man. Christie smiled back, more of relief he was ok. Tez pulled a face.

"Babe, why you wearing that?" he asked.

"Because you have my stuff on," she said with a flirty smile.

In the light of the kitchen Tez realised he had his jeans on, but her pink top, that was very short. Phipps laughed until it became a racking cough, red faced, eyes streaming. Christie stood beside Tez and touched him playfully.

"You know, I like girls too," she said, stroking his exposed stomach. Tez slapped her hand away, pulled her top off and gave it too her. Phipps wiped his eyes, hoping she would change there, but she winked at him and walked away, pulling the shirt over her head. Phipps tried to watch but Tez blocked the view. He'd gotten the old first aid kit from the kitchen cupboards and was looking at the cut on the old farmers head.

"Not bad," Tez said, taking a bandage and making a pad from it to hold over the wound. "Best get it checked though." Phipps waved him away. "Sod me, what about your car?"

Tez smiled, unwrapping another bandage to hold the pad in place. He spoke as he wound it around the greying head.

"All the cars are fine. I knew he'd do something like this, so I moved everything."

"You moved them?" asked Phipps, wincing at the pain.

"Yep." Tez stood back and looked at the old man. He

seemed clear headed and alert, but you couldn't be sure. "How did you know he wouldn't go after you?"

Tez smiled, poured a glass of water, and handed it to the man.

"I knew. He wants to see me fail. The only way to do that is to remove my ability to beat him. No car means I lose. No me means no bet. He wants me and Christie alive and well so he can gloat." Tez looked out the window. The shed was now a smouldering pile of twisted beams, molten metal and smoke. Blue lights came up the drive, flashing like a slot machine. "I think until the big day I may have to vanish," Tez said absently, watching the black shape of Henderson's Range Rover park next to Phipps's tatty old Land Rover.

They took the old farmer to hospital to treat his head. Aside from a nasty gash to the back of his head he was fine, but they wanted him in overnight for observation because of his age. Tez wasn't too keen to see the inside of another hospital ward, Christie even less so. As two young nurses tucked the old man into bed he still kept his humour and wit, asking for different parts to be adjusted for him, enjoying the attention.

"And I think I may need a sponge bath," he said in a dirty voice, winking at the prettier of the two nurses.

She smiled back and patted his hand. "I'm sure our poor old soldier can get a bed bath. I'll get it sorted for you now," she whispered almost seductively. Phipps nearly giggled, wiggling his feet in anticipation. The nurse left, saying softly "shame it will be a male nurse doing it," as she passed Tez, who smiled.

Shutting the door Tez sat on the vinyl hospital chair, noticing they were as uncomfortable as the intensive care wards, and looked at the man so out of place in the white hospital bed. Christie stayed by the door, as if afraid to approach the same type of bed she had spent so long in.

Tez sighed and shrugged. Phipps winked at him.

"So, kid. Where did you hide my cars?"

"Safe," said Tez. "Don't worry about them, just get out of here, and I'll tell you when you get home."

"Clever. What you gonna do now?"

Tez dropped his head. "What I should have done years ago. I shouldn't have come to you. I'll pay for your shed."

Phipps waved a hand. "Don't worry. I had it insured anyway. May make a bit of a claim there was some valuables in there."

Tez nodded. "I'm still sorry. I just wish this was over."

"Give it a week kid, then you'll feel better."

Tez smiled. "Or worse."

Phipps sat up sharply and gripped the young man's wrist with surprising strength. "Don't say that. You'll wipe the ass off that git. You will. Have faith."

"You'll win, babe," said Christie, still loitering by the door.

"Yeah," sighed Tez, sitting back down when Phipps let him go. "Just know from the past you can go in with everything perfect, and lose it on anything."

"True," said Phipps. "But that's life. Believe."

"I'll try. And you believe in your sponge bath." Tez patted his arm as the man giggled.

"Wonder how transparent those uniforms get when they get damp?" he mused. Tez laughed, and Christie joined in.

The door opened, making them all look. Henderson came in with two uniformed officers, both burly and muscular. The laugh died on the old man's lips. Henderson sat on the other chair, ignoring the patient, looking at Tez.

"So, Belkin, what you planning?"

"Not much, copper," said Tez. "Gonna go underground for the week. Some place safe."

Henderson shook his head, and waved at the two behind him. "These 'gentlemen' are for your protection. You're now on the witness protection plan. They'll guard you and your car."

Tez looked the men over, and laughed. "Thanks, but no thanks. I know a place. I spent many years evading the law. I doubt they can help against guys who do the same."

Henderson looked pained. "These chaps are the two best self defence security experts in the force. I had to pull a lot of strings to get them."

"Then twang your strings and take them back. I got this."

Christie watched with confusion as they almost squared off over the prostrate body of Phipps, who pretended to be asleep with a cheeky smile on his wrinkled lips.

Henderson stood. "You need protection, and you're gonna get it."

Tez leant back, calm. "I need to vanish. Can't do that with two coppers on my bumper."

"You won't see them."

Tez stood too, patted the old man's hand and smiled. "True. I won't. If they can keep up, they can come with." He nodded and left. Christie followed. Henderson looked down to the sleeping Phipps.

"Get to walking, copper," said Phipps between fake snores. Henderson smiled and left.

25

Tez drove late, the stripped out Volvo wasn't really

suited to long distance driving, but they managed. At least the engine Tez made was super efficient, so fuel stops were out of the equation. Christie kept silent, letting him handle the big car as it bounced around the back roads, avoiding motorways and main streets. None looked familiar to her, having never gone more then an hour from home except on a plane for holidays. When you have a pub you are kind of anchored to it.

Tez knew where he was going. The roads became more familiar, the scenery, the buildings, all he knew. Finally they came to a tiny village of red brick houses. Stopping outside one Tez left the engine running, but got out. The house was a large detached with ivy growing over the narrow porch, a nicely tended garden and a small metal gate leading from the street. The low red brick wall surrounded the garden, and ended at the side of the house where a larger wooden gate opened to a tarmac drive around the back. It was this gate he opened, getting back into the car and driving in.

At the end of the drive was a large garage, well lit with a ramp and almost clinically clean. The floor was painted red, walls and ceiling white. On the ramp was a pure track car, stripped out and lightened. A man was working under the car, a young woman helping him, passing tools like a nurse in an operation. They both heard the Volvo's exhaust, but only the girl looked. She was shocked at first, then disgusted. She dropped the tools she was holding back into an open cabinet, and stormed off.

Tez stopped by the garage and killed the engine. Christie noticed the pained, almost upset look and was worried. He got out the car, took a deep breath, and joined the man.

Both stood together looking at the underside of the car on the ramp.

"So," said the man.

"Yeah," replied Tez.

Christie got out and stood by the car, watching.

"Knew you'd come back," said the man, not doing anything on the car, but still looking intently at it.

"Yeah. Had to," Tez said.

"Well, now you can go."

Tez dropped his head. "I can't."

"Oh yes you can. You did before, remember?" The man reached past him and selected a spanner.

"I know. I was a dick. But I've changed." "Really?" asked the man.

"Yeah. I have. Got a job, a flat," he paused and looked back to Christie with a haunted face, "a girl."

The man still didn't turn. "A job? At a place that mysteriously was blown up by a car bomb?"

Tez looked stunned. "How?"

The man dropped the spanner back into the chest. Tez unconsciously put it neatly in the drawer rack with the others. The man sat on a battered settee by the side of the garage. Tez sat beside him, opened a small fridge beside the settee and took out two cans. Opening one he passed it to the man, then opened the other.

"Think I'd let my own son vanish and not keep an eye on him. Lower Hampton, right?"

"Yeah." Tez smiled despite the mixed emotions he felt.

"I know all about you, son. I know you changed. A new leaf you could say. But I know what follows you. I want to help, but I can't have you here."

"Dad, why not?"

"Because I don't want this falling down on your mum and sister. Do you?"

Tez shook his head, and took a long draw from the can. Christie watched with fascination, noticing the girl watching her from the back door of the house. She inspected Christie's clothes, figure, attitude with intense concentration. When she realised she was spotted she made a face of extreme irritation and left, watching through a window instead.

"Dad, I gotta do this. One last time."

"You should have stayed on the track, son." His father took a draw and shook his head. "Could have been rich and successful."

"I couldn't, dad. You know they banned the car."

"Damn the car. This is your future. Work for a normal team. You can still do it. Why run?"

Tez shrugged. "I don't know. But I do know I want to stop running."

His father drained his can and threw it over arm into a metal bin, bouncing off the back wall first. Tez did the same, getting it perfectly in the centre. He went for another can, but a hand stopped him.

"Can't let you drink and drive, son," said his dad.

Tez looked pleadingly at him. "I gotta find a place, just for a week. I need to prep the car, get sorted. I gotta beat this guy, Dad."

"Why? Why the need to race all of a sudden? Why not just walk away?"

"Walking is just running, but slower. If I don't beat this guy he'll never stop looking."

His dad looked him in the eye for the first time. "And what makes you think he will stop if you win?"

Tez smiled. "Plan. I ain't doing this alone. Got everything sorted, just need a place to hide for a week."

His dad stood and held out a hand. Tez took it, stood and smiled, eyes getting moist.

"Sorry son, but you can't stay here."

Tez almost cried. Christie wanted to go hold him, but

felt almost pushed away.

"You can't stay here," his dad said again, "but I can help."

Tez smiled, the tears finally falling. His father pulled out a set of keys from a box in the garage and threw them over. Tez caught them and looked in surprise.

"Yeah," said his dad, nodding. "It's your old truck. Kept the thing, even gave it a go over. Knew you'd come back. Take the car trailer. Hide your car, and turn up to your race like a proper racer."

Tez broke from himself, starting at a run around the garage, skidding to a stop, and doubling back. He nearly flattened his dad in a massive bear hug, making the older version of Tez smile in spite of the past tension. Tez took off again, waving Christie to follow. She left the car grudgingly and passed the father of her man.

"I'm Christine by the way," she said weakly.

"I'm glad," said the man with a friendly smile, then he went back to his work.

Behind the garage was a small concrete parking place for three cars. One was empty, another had a large blue covered car trailer, the kind you can use to tow a race car anywhere, with tools and spares in. The last space had an old Land Rover, like the one Phipps used on his farm. This one was a little different. It was raised slightly, with an external roll cage, metal plates all around the edges, lights and a raised air intake. Tez was standing in front of it, shaking his head but laughing.

"Hey, babe," he said as Christie hooked an arm around his waist. "You know, I built this when I was fourteen to tow the trailer and help recover wrecks from the track. Can't believe it's still here."

Tez pulled the Land Rover forwards, Christie wasn't surprised it had a loud V8 in it, and connected the trailer.

Checking all the lights worked and the tyres were ok he got the Volvo and drove it into the trailer. Satisfied all was secure Tez got in the Land Rover, waited for Christie to join him, and smiled.

"On the road again," he said, in almost a sing song voice.

They drove past the garage, where his dad ignored them, and out onto the street. Christie jumped out to close the gate while Tez manoeuvred the long car and trailer through the tight street. Back inside she put her belt on and touched his thigh softly.

"So, where now?" she asked.

"Back to my old haunts, and see if my fellow spooks still haunt them," Tez said. Leaving the old brick house they drove away, hoping they were now truly hidden from unwanted eyes.

26

The traffic light blazed red. Below two cars, one a very shiny deep red, the other a dull matte black, waited. Side by side they revved the engines, loud exhausts competing for who was loudest. On the pavement by the crossroads people cheered, shouted, called and insulted the two drivers. The red light was joined by the yellow light below.
Both cars sat in the power band, ready. Green light.

With a screech of tyres and small flames popping from the large exhaust pipes both cars fired down the street, the cheers from the onlookers drowned in the noise. One stepped out after the smoke had cleared and held up a hand.

"Ok, ok. Wow!. That is how we do it." He lifted a walkie talkie to his lips. "Well?"

"Red Civic, but only just," came the tinny answer. The crowd cheered louder, some groaning as money was exchanged. The red Honda came back first, the black Ford Focus second. The cars stopped by the kerb, engines off. The man with the radio shook both their hands, then the two racers shook each other's, passing a small wad of cash from red to black.

"Ok, people. Time to go," the first said. They were about to leave when the sound of a tuned car made them stop and look. The silver Volvo looked familiar, but only a few could be sure. When it stopped nose to nose with the Honda nobody moved.

Tez got out very reluctantly. This was really scraping the bottom of the barrel. Christie felt the unease, but still got out as well, standing by her man. Tez looked at the small crowd, trying to read their mood. The short dumpy man in the red Honda spoke first.

"Ah, hell no," he said, getting into his car and driving away with far more vigour then needed. The tyre smoke drifted through the crowd. The man with the radio stepped forwards until he stood in front of the Volvo.

"Really?" he asked.

Tez shrugged.

The man looked over the car. "After all these years you come back? Got a lot of balls after what happened."

"And if I hadn't gone? Asked Tez.

The man stopped beside Tez. "True." He suddenly grabbed Tez in a massive man hug. Tez took a moment to recover, then returned the embrace. Christie smiled in relief as the bad vibes melted.

"Hey, Babe," said Tez to Christie. "This is my old racing buddy, Ricky Howell. He used to run number two for me."

"Never could beat this old tank," said Ricky with a laugh.

"And is that little Tommy?" asked Tez, breaking free from Ricky and giving the gangly driver of the Ford another man hug. Tom giggled like a small boy, and bent slightly to pat Tez on the back.

"So, TB, this old tank still got it?" asked Ricky.

"You wanna find out?" asked Tez.

Ricky nodded, turned and walked away. Tez got back in his car and drove to the lights. An old white Ford Escort RS turbo warbled alongside. Both looked at each other and laughed. Windows rolled down so they could talk.

"Like old times?" asked Tez.

"Yeah, except this time I'm gonna hand your ass back to you," replied Ricky.

"You wish," said Tez.

The lights turned red, windows went up, and both cars begin building the revs. Amber came, and Ricky did a burnout to warm his tyres. Tez just waited. Green and both cars took off. They were side by side for the start, then Tez looked to Ricky, smiled, and suddenly the gap between them grew as the Volvo powered away. Tez crossed the spray painted finish line a clear three car lengths ahead.

Back at the lights Christie felt alone in the crowd. When the Volvo came back she nearly ran back to it, to safety. Tez parked in front of the Focus, Ricky parking his Escort in front.

"Damn, TB," said Ricky. "What the hell have you done to that thing? Sure I would whip you this time."

Tez laughed and leant on the side of his car. "Time made you soft," he said.

Ricky shook his hand. "Good race. Anyway, why are

you back?"

Tez winked. "Is Peter's still open?"

"Best kebab in town? Sure."

"I'm hungry," said Tez, getting back into his car.

Peter's Fish and Chip Shop was famous locally for the food, but also Russell Peters, who was more than a character. When he saw Tez walk in he vaulted the counter, nearly flattened two customers, and floored Tez, sitting on him like a wrestler.

"Hey, Belkin. Why you go? Got boring here without you." "Sorry, Russ," said Tez, struggling to breathe.

Peters stood, helped the young man to his feet, and vaulted the counter again. Ignoring everyone else he made a massive donner kebab and flung it to Tez. For a man getting close to sixty Peters was the image of a lithe athletic sportsman. he played cricket for the local team, was an ex badminton champ and could win at most pub quizzes on sports. He leant on the counter away from the till, letting his staff serve the customers. As Tez ate his kebab Peters kept taking it off him, topping up the pitta bread, passing it back.

"So good to see you again," he said.

Tez nodded, munching kebab. Christie tried a strip, stated it was indeed the best she'd tasted, and found another white paper wrapped kebab landing on her lap.

Ricky caught his kebab and the three of them sat at the small wooden table while they ate.

"So then, boss. Why you back here?" asked Ricky.

"Trouble," said Tez, thanking Peters when his kebab was refilled.

"What else."

Tez shook his head. "Big trouble." He explained what had happened after he left, drifting, finding a new home, meeting Christie, the Hopwood brothers, the grudge match, the car bomb. Ricky listened with mounting concern, Peters stopped refilling kebabs and listened too. At the end Ricky pushed his half full kebab away.

"Wow. You really are a magnet for crap," he said.

"Found you twice," said Tez.

"Touché," said Ricky. "But seriously, what you gonna do?"

"Race the git, and beat him. Saw yourself the car is perfect. Never been better. He has a Skyline with way too much power, but he knows how to use it. He can't race dirty, so unless he stops me getting on that start line he'll lose."

Ricky looked to the ceiling for a moment. "You need to go to ground?"

"Yeah," said Tez.

Ricky looked worried briefly, then smiled. "Think we can hide you," he said, pulled his kebab closer and resumed eating. Tez smiled back, held out a hand and shook.

"Good to be home," Tez said, and after giving Christie a greasy kiss on the cheek he tucked back into his kebab. Christie just ate in silence, confused, but confident in Tez's ability to keep her safe.

The bond between Tez and Ricky was obvious from the start, but the past left a stain. Under the brotherly love and macho bull the pain from history still tugged on them both. They kept up the banter while they ate, but once the paper was empty, even with the constant refills, Tez stood and walked out, followed by Ricky. Christie felt like a fifth wheel still, but she left too, giving them space.

Behind the takeaway was a narrow alley, leading to a tiny car park next to a kids playground. Both men sat on the swings, idly kicking their legs to make them move together.

"So, what happened, boss?" asked Ricky.

Tez sighed, leant back to swing higher. "I had to go. You know that."

"Hell yeah I know that. If you hadn't we'd be swinging in the nick instead of out here. Full of convict man juice, instead of sheep's brains. I get why you left. Now I wanna know why you came back. The real reason. Not for a reunion, that's for damn sure."

"Nah. Not a reunion. Got trouble."

Ricky shrugged, and tried to swing higher than Tez, making it a small race. "Figured it was something like that. You racing again?"

"This time I didn't even do anything," said Tez. Ricky paused for a moment, then resumed kicking and leaning in the rubber swing seat.

"Nothing?" Ricky asked, nodding to Christie, who was hiding near the alley entrance, watching two grown men play like kids.

"Nothing. Some local arse hole wants to rule the world. His brother won't let him, so they fight. Guy wants my car so he can win. Other guy don't want him to have it. So I get stuck in the middle."

Ricky listened with interest. They used to get into trouble before, but usually for what they did and they expected it. This was purely passive, and for Ricky that never happened.

"So he wants your car. Why you gotta run? You can beat any damn thing short of a Hellfire missile." Ricky was winning the competition so Tez leant back farther, closing the gap before he spoke. They had to near shout with the effort, noise and distance as they swung.

"Not a simple call out. He wants to race in a grudge match, in front of everyone. I win, he goes bye-bye. He wins and I lose it all, including Christie."

Ricky slammed his feet onto the worn tarmac below the swing.

"You bet your girl?"

Tez didn't respond, just waited until he had swung to furthest forwards, then jumped, carrying on his arc until he landed on one knee like Superman. He turned back to Ricky and shrugged.

"If I don't bury him in front of everyone he'll keep pushing. I can and will beat that twat, but I need to do it next Saturday. He wants me to lose, but knows he can't beat me straight up, so he will try every trick in the book to stop me."

Ricky got off the swing, stretching and rubbing the feeling back into his ass. "So if you don't show you forfeit?"

"Got it in one," said Tez.

"You want to hide," said Ricky, thinking.

Tez smiled, letting his friend think through what Tez had already planned.

"Hey," said Ricky. "Why not stay with us? Like the old days. We can really get your car set up properly, and you can turn up in style?"

"Thanks for the invite, but I can't have you coming with me. If this does go tits up I need somewhere secret to hide and make my return. Just a roof and some ramp time will be enough."

Ricky stood before his old friend, almost looking like he would lash out with a fist. Instead he grabbed Tez and pulled him into a massive bear hug. Tez felt the air knocked out of him, but managed a weak return to the man hug.

"You are always welcome," said Ricky, breaking the embrace. Tez shook his hand, waved to Christie to join them, and the three of them went back to their cars. The fox had gone to ground.

27

The house, small and unimpressive from the front, stood at the end of the row. Concrete prefabricated in the 60's for the local council it had three windows overlooking the street, and an unremarkable front door. Down the side was a neat and smooth concrete drive. Behind was a different story. This was why the house had 'Tardis' on the front door.

The back opened onto a massive yard, easily big enough to be a small car park. Four garage units lined both sides, and at the end was a two storey block with roller shutter doors opening to three car bays, with rooms upstairs to sleep, shower, cook and a massive games room. Floor mounted glass panels let those upstairs see the bays and the cars below. Ricky showed Christie around, letting her settle in the larger bedroom and get cleaned up. He and Tez headed out to the yard. The Volvo was unloaded from the car trailer, which they hid beside the workshop. The Land Rover was parked on the other side, by the fire exit, just in case. The Volvo was put on the first ramp, and with Ricky and some extra help it was soon in bits and spread out all over the floor, every component being checked over.

"Bad news," said Tom Howards. "You got a stress fracture in the block."

Tez cursed and looked past Tom's head torch at the dark grey carbon engine. Faintly on one of the mounting points he could see a fine hairline crack. Ricky came over to look, and they both exchanged and glance and shook their heads.

"No good?" asked Tom.

"Nope," said Tez. "May hold, but it could break when I put full boost on. Mostly I have the turbo off, and the fuel map on low power. For this I need full bore and that can't break."

Ricky looked at it again. "Can't we fix it?"

"Can't weld carbon ceramic," said Tez "So what we do?" asked Tom.

Tez smiled, a smile they used to know, especially when fishing for easy money races. "I think we need another one."

Professor Jerome Bertram loved history. He lived it, he breathed it. If anyone asked him a history question they would soon wish they hadn't. But a small portion in the annals or more recent history recorded the tomfoolery of two of his worst pupils. Had the come back to haunt him?

"Young Belkin, Howell," he said, even though there wasn't much difference in their ages, Bertram was a student teacher when he taught them.

"Hey Mr Bertram," said Tez.

"Well?" asked Bertram.

"Is your science lab still well equipped?"

Bertram looked puzzled, but nodded. "I believe so. They added a new forming kiln that's supposed to be better then the old one, but besides that it should be all the same. Why?"

"Just wondering," said Tez. "Looking over the old school."

"Yes, I'll bet. Don't steal anything, please," said Bertram, and watched them leave. His head said to stop them, but his gut said to let them be. He listened to his gut and opened his pad, resuming his latest textbook.

The science lab was cleaner, but more cluttered than when they last used it. Tez moved with his usual comfortable motion. Ricky was more hesitant.

"You really know what you're doing?" he asked Tez, looking in a microscope.

"Sure. Done it before." Tez checked over the kiln, familiarising himself with the controls.

"So how do you make an engine?" asked Ricky, looking over his shoulder at Tez.

"Takes a day of baking, then a couple of days cleaning it up, and some milling."

"You got the plans?"

Tez tapped his head. "Always."

Leaving Ricky to examine a wall chart of chemical elements Tez sat at a computer terminal. With a rapid machine gun of key clicks the 3D printer next door whirred into life, making a white frame that slowly became an engine block. Tez checked it looked right, then started a complicated process of covering it with clay. Once happy with the results he put the brown lump into the now hot kiln. It had become dark outside so they closed the blinds and worked on. Ricky was tasked with watching the time for the kiln, and finding enough carbon and other ingredients while Tez made another block from the printer and covered it in clay. Once the first was ready he swapped them over, letting the hot one cool down. With care Tez made a hole until he reached the cavity where the 3d print had been, now burnt out from the kiln.

Tez put the clay back in while he mixed a strange potion in a large bowl, the smell making Ricky feel sick and tired. With another hole in the clay mould and the mould itself reheated, Tez warmed the mix on the clay, then poured it slowly into the larger hole. Hot air blew from the other hole as the mix filled the mould. Once full Tez nodded and wearing thick gloves both carried it back into the kiln.

They repeated the process with the second block, then, once all was cleaned up and hidden, they slipped out the way they used to when they skipped school, leaving the moulds to cure in the kiln.

Two days later, and some grazes from the frantic escape from the school, Tez lay the two dull grey lumps on the garage floor. The striped engine lay next to them, laid out ready for assembly. Tex had managed to machine the blocks to his standards, which is how they nearly got caught. Both now had five smooth bores for the pistons, milled to the exact size needed. The mating faces for the head and sump were also smoothed to a perfect flat edge. The mounts were in the perfect place, all the bolt holes tapped, they were ready.

Ricky had forgotten how skilled and clever Tez was. He managed from memory to build two identical engine blocks, using unfamiliar equipment, and making the actual engines from a chemical mix nobody else knew. He knew the sizes of the bolts used, the piston dimensions and where to fit everything. The test fit of the engines and the parts inside had been perfect. Both were equally exact. But Tez wasn't happy. He went over both on engine stands, turning over repeatedly, checking and rechecking with an LED torch. He muttered to himself, grunting, and letting the odd low curse slip. Christie watched her man frown and sigh as he bent over the two engines. She knew why, but it was still a concern.

"Boss," said Ricky eventually. "They're both perfect. We can use either."

Tez waved him away, taking a pair of digital vernier callipers and going over the blocks again. Short of getting a magnifying glass he spent three hours using most of the inspection tools in the workshop, before he stood, groaned at the ache in his back and touched one of the blocks.

"This one," he said.

The guys leapt into action, getting ready as Tez himself selected tools like a surgeon, carefully fitting new bearings, checking parts and new seals. An hour later the engine was ready. The engine was so light it took two of them to line it up in the engine bay by hand, while Tez lay underneath checking the clutch. Once the fuel lines, coolant and electrics were connected, with the key in one hand, and fingers crossed on the other, Tez fired it up. It ran a little rough, clicking and vibrating, but Tez let it idle for a few minutes and the engine smoothed out slowly. After a fifteen minute run he turned it off, and let the guys change the oil from the expensive wear-in oil, to the racing grade. Ricky watched them do it.

"This gonna work, boss?" he asked.

Tez nodded. "We gotta let it bed in properly, check the turbo is running right, get it up to temperature and boost. Could do with a dyno test too."

Ricky nodded. "That's easy. Got a rolling road out back. Use it for pre race bets."

"Get it," said Tez.

"Thought you wanted it to bed in?"

"No time like the present." Tez watched as the car was lowered to the ground, bonnet refitted. He got in, reversed off the ramp and pulled up next to the open trailer that had the dyno mounted in it. Ricky set the dyno up while Tez did some short practice runs around the yard. When he was done Ricky waved Tez over and began strapping the car to the dyno.

"What's going on?" asked Christie.

"Checking the power of the car," said Ricky, setting the program on the dyno computer. "How?"

"Never seen a dyno run?"

Christie shook her head.

"Watch," said Ricky.

Three big red numbers appeared above the monitor. The first was zero, the other two hovering around the 30 mark.

Christie realised it was the speed the wheels were turning. Tez was fiddling with something inside the car. The exhaust note changed suddenly, from the familiar warble to a deep rasp. Ricky waved a hand, then put them both over his ears. Christie did the same as Tez hit the go pedal. The numbers shot up, past 40 and rising fast. Soon it was over 100, engine screaming. Small flames shot from the wide exhaust pipe as the car strained against the thick straps holding it to the dyno. With a rapid fire from the exhaust Tez hit the limit and pulled off the accelerator. The numbers dropped a lot slower than they rose. Letting the car idle in neutral Tez leant out the window and shouted to Ricky.

Ricky just shook his head, smiling.

"Come on," called Tez.

"What did it used to do?" asked Ricky.

"About 350 brake before."

"Ah, cool."

Tez resisted the urge to hit his old friend. Instead he gestured for him to carry on.

"You know that bet?" Ricky asked, dragging it out.

"Yeah?" said Tez.

"I should double it," said Ricky, laughing.

"Why? What was it?"

Ricky struggled to speak through his laughter. "Four hundred and thirty-three," he said finally.

Tez looked shocked.

"Four thirty-three?" he asked.

Ricky nodded, and showed the read out.

"Well, we can beat that," smiled Tez, patted the steering wheel and let Ricky set up the dyno again.

They tested for over half an hour, changing fuel ratios, turbo boost, and even considering nitrous. With the car's small race tank getting low they called it a day, worried the noise would give them away.

"Doubt it," said Ricky "We do a lot of pre race testing here. The locals know all about it. But can't be too careful."

The dyno was packed away, car hidden inside for another oil change, and Tez went to bed happy. After a while Christie let him sleep.

Henderson sat at his desk thinking. He hadn't heard from the kid in days. The grudge match was only four days away, and with the utmost secrecy Henderson had organised an elite team of pursuit drivers to be ready with the best patrol cars for the arrest of Colin. He knew the younger of the two brothers was the one who torched the pub, attacked the garage, and probably put the Thorpe family in the hospital. He just had to find the link. Concrete evidence meant assured convictions. Any police officer will testify the worst part of the job is when you know who did it, but the court let them walk. It had happened five years before, when the big riot turned the market place into a war zone. Colin walked then due to 'insufficient evidence'. Henderson nearly went for the judge. Instead he bided his time, waiting.

Now he'd filled his tiny office with two massive white boards, covered the walls with papers and photo's pinned with red string linking them. He didn't go out, even for coffee. Instead, like a mathematician trying to solve a complex equation, Henderson sat at his desk and stared at the mess, trying to find the pattern like a magic eye picture.

He felt grimy, tired and irritable. The bit that made it worse was the knowledge he had no time to solve it, and get ready.

There was an almost apologetic knock at the door and Constable Bicks came in, holding a giant mug of coffee. Henderson waved her away, but she came in, squatted beside the table and placed the mug before him like a lackey to a master. Henderson grunted something, and without looking away from his papers he took the mug. One sip and his eyes opened briefly, and he looked at the still crouching constable. She smiled, nodded, and gently laid a hand on his knee.

Without saying any more she stood, and looked around at the jumble of string and push pins. Henderson watched her, seeing her with new light. Something stirred inside, fuelled by the best coffee he's ever tasted. Bicks turned around twice, slowly, taking it all in. then she paced the four walls, inspecting all the images and reports. To Henderson's horror she began pulling the string off. He was about to speak, half raised from his seat, when Bicks held out a string covered hand, and carried on. Three minutes later and the string was back, in a different way. Henderson stood fully, and stared. The rookie had solved the maths equation for him.

Linking the attacks, the explosions, and the riots, were only three people. One was Ricky Robins, who Colin had thrown out recently, Martin Stone, his right hand man, and Rich, Henderson's mole. The info Rich had given him showed they were involved in the theft of the bomb car, Colin had experience in explosives when he used to work briefly at an open face mine, and the vague description from a shop girl put him in place buying the bomb items. Stone had stolen the car, the Skyline was close enough to the blurred CCTV images to place them both. The riot camera shots were old and grainy, but the trademark white hoodie Colin always wore was there in the centre. That was the key. He never let anyone else wear one like his, it was his talisman. His stocky, muscular build made it hard to mistake him.

Henderson looked at Bicks with a mix of awe and irritation. She smiled, paused, then gave him a kiss on the cheek. He smelt her perfume, the shampoo in her long blonde hair, the subtle scent of lunch on her breath. Bicks left, leaving Henderson confused, excited, aroused and panicking at the same time. Shaking all over like a dog drying itself he went back to his desk and shoved some space clear in the mound of paperwork. Taking a clean sheet of paper he formed his draft request. He had four days to convince the clerk of the court to grant him a warrant for Colin Hopwood's arrest, and get his men ready.

Four days and it will all be over.

28

Tez rolled over in bed, making Christie moan in irritation. He felt her reach out under the blanket, touch his back, arm curling around his waist and pulling him closer. He felt the firmness of her breasts on his shoulders, her breath on his neck, her feet on the back of his knees. The arm wandered over his stomach, tracing the faint outlines of muscles, up to his chest, playfully passing over his nipples. The hand then wandered down, pausing briefly on his lower belly, until it reached his crotch. It seemed happy with what it found as it didn't wander any more. Tez grunted, then rolled back to face her. That sleepy, but flirty look was in her eyes, the 'come to bed' face. Tez gave in easily and wrapped his legs around hers, letting his own hands play up and down her back and she wriggled and moaned.

There was a knock at the door.

Tez tried to pull away but Christie wouldn't let him, clamping his body to her. The knock came louder. Tez was about to shout to whoever it was to go, although that would have been hard with Christie's tongue in his mouth, when the door frame splintered around the lock and the door flew open. Such was the force the door actually closed again, much to the anger of the kicker. When the door opened again it was for the last time as the hinges gave. Colin Hopwood looked at the bed and near screamed in rage. It was empty.

In the next room Tez and Christie had hurriedly dressed and dropped out the back window. Why Colin had gone for that door and not the bedroom next to it Tez didn't know, but he wasn't gonna go back and ask. Peering around the corner of the workshop garage he saw the yard was full of 4power cars. They'd found him. The Land Rover was too far, and the trailer even farther. No escape. The high wall around the yard backed onto alleyways and gardens, too tall to climb and with the only entrance blocked with cars they could never make it on foot.

Inside more bangs and shouts indicated the path of a rampaging Colin. A window smashed above, scattering glass shards on the dirt behind them. Hidden by a storage locker Colin couldn't see them, but he knew they were somewhere here.

"Tez!" he yelled. "You come out, or I torch this place!"

Christie looked terrified, knowing Colin's anger first

hand.

Tez looked impressively calm. There was almost a smile. Christie gave him a shocked look, and he actually winked. Then, to her horror, he stood and walked around the side of the garage to face the gang waiting. Numbly she followed. "Hey guys," Tez called amiably. "Wassup?"

Martin waited with his arms folded over his chest, almost as surprised as Christie. Some of the guys noticed she was half dressed, a miss-buttoned short shirt and denim shorts, no shoes and make up. Tez still faced them all, a smile on his face like a friendly host at a party.

"Wassup?" asked a menacing voice behind. Colin stood almost like an angry bear, panting, red faced. "You," he started, then paused, unsure what to do. He'd expected to find them asleep, batter them both and take the car. But they were both up and dressed, sort of, and being nice.

"Hey, Colin. Ready for the race tomorrow?" Tez asked. The only way he could be nicer would have been to offer a cup of tea and shake his hand. Confusion passed over Colin's face like waves, fuelling his anger.

"Race?" Colin asked.

"Yeah. You know?" Big race tomorrow?" Tez kept the happy charade up. Inside his mind was already racing. Contrary to outward impressions he'd planned the escape route years before. Now he just needed one thing to flee.

Colin was getting more than a little frustrated, torn between the kindness of his enemy, and the anger he felt towards this little rat. Behind Colin the rest of his gang were getting unsettled, seeing their decisive leader reduced to stutters and mumbles. Martin went to touch Colin's arm, then stopped himself in case Colin turned on him. Instead he coughed loudly. Colin shook his head, clearing it.

"There ain't gonna be a race tomorrow," Colin said,

regaining his composure. "Not between us, anyway."

"Aww, shame," said Tez, still grinning. "Was looking forwards to it. You come to say you're backing out? Easier ways than this."

"Backing out? I'm not backing out. I never run. Not like some. You won't be racing, unless you're good with a wheelchair."

"I'm not bad," said Tez. "But why a chair?"

"'Cos I'm gonna break both your legs, then take your little slut back with me and break her."

Christie gasped softly, and held back the tears. Tez noticed she was being strong for him, and that made him smile even more.

"Why you grinning, dick?" asked Colin.

Tez shrugged. "I suppose because life is good. And I'm gonna enjoy this bit."

Colin flinched back in shock. "You enjoy pain?"

"Not really," Tez admitted. "But if you want some, I can give you some."

Christie, later on, couldn't remember clearly what happened next. It was a blur, like the morning after the night before. She saw Colin launch himself at her man, Tez sidestepped last second, spun, then Colin was on the floor, crying out in pain. Tez grabbed her arm so hard it left a bruise, and pulled her towards the brick wall behind the garage. Pausing briefly he pushed a brick and a section swung out into the back alley. Once through he pushed it back. As they hurried away Christie saw the wall had no marks, no sign it was actually a gate. On the other side Colin roared in rage and shrieked for everyone to go find them.

Seeing the glow on his face Christie once again marvelled at the mind of her man, and felt her love grow even more. Dashing down back alleys she stopped him, pointing at her naked feet. Tez bowed low like a butler, and charged at her. Grabbing her like a rugby tackle he picked her up on his shoulder in a fireman's lift and kept running.

Bouncing on his shoulder Christie looked back the way they had come, Colin's shouts fading.

Saturday came, warm and still. The residents of Lower Hampton knew their past, remembered what had been before. The shops were closed, streets empty. The town was like a ghost town. Nothing moved.

From the street outside Colin Hopwood's house the deep base tone of a line of floor hugging race cars bounced from wall to wall. With a hand signal through an open window the leaf scraping convoy headed out, curtains twitching as they passed. The line drove to the main south road, and passed the Black Bull pub, still boarded up. Taking the narrow country lanes they arrived at the old aerodrome and lined up on the concrete.

At the same time the higher whine of motorbike engines echoed from the biker workshop in the northern end of the town, forming a staggered train of bikes that rolled slowly through deserted streets. Once at the aerodrome they lined up opposite the cars, two lines of warriors ready for battle.

In the back of the police station to the east the black hulk of Henderson's Range Rover waited idly, the big V8 rumbling softly to itself. In the driver's seat Henderson picked his mobile phone from the cubby hole above the radio and pressed speed dial. It rang once then answered.

"Ready?" asked Henderson.

"Yeah. You?" said the phone.

"Let's go," answered Henderson. He put the phone back, leant out the open window and waved. Filling the enclosed yard behind the Police station were several marked performance police cars, two riot vans and even more marked normal patrol cars. The uniformed officers in body armour nodded at the signal, got into their cars and waited.

29

Colin got out of his car, making it look like a chore he was forced to perform. With reluctance he faced his brother, who irritated him by smiling.

"We really doing this?" asked Mark, unzipping his leather jacket. The warm breeze stirred his ponytail, making Colin shudder in rage.

"Yeah, dumbass. We are doing this." Colin smiled suddenly, horribly. "Unless you wanna chicken out again, pussy."

Mark smiled back, and shook his head. "Nah. This won't take long."

"Not long at all," said Colin.

They both stood side by side, with an obvious gap left between them. After an uncomfortable exchange of glances Mark spoke first.

"So, you know the rules. Anyone wants to call off?"

One of the 4power drivers stepped from his car.

"No way," he said. "I'm still calling out Red Head there."

The ginger haired biker bristled slightly, then shrugged. "Sure. Shame it isn't someone who's a challenge."

The driver tensed, then opened his mouth to speak. Mark interrupted him.

"Hey, save it, guys. Anyone else?"

One by one everyone confirmed their grudges, making

bets on the races, some for money, some for more. Once everyone had finished Mark turned to his brother.

"Suppose you are throwing it in too?" he asked.

"You bet," said Colin. "And same stakes too."

Mark shook his head, held out a hand and they shook on it.

"Locked in," said Mark. They turned back to face the two ranks when the sound of loud exhausts stopped them. A small convoy of cars was driving to the aerodrome. Through the narrow gate came the red Corsa driven by Christie, the old Land Rover driven by Phipps, three street racers they didn't recognise, and the silver and black Volvo with Tez. They drove to the group, parking in a line at right angles so from above the groups looked like the symbol for pi.

Tez got out, having parked in the middle, and fist pumped with Ricky, Tom and Mick. Christie stood beside her man, wearing a short skirt but a big, padded jacket, looking warm in the sun. Mark shook his head, amused. His brother went pink in anger.

"What the hell are you doing here, prick?" Colin spat at Tez.

Tez coughed loudly when Ricky went to move forwards, and looked at the concrete road below him. He idly scuffed his trainers on the mottled surface, as if thinking of what to say. He then looked up to the sparse clouds, examining the blue sky. Colin was about to speak when Tez suddenly walked towards him with such purpose Mark nearly moved away.

"Well," said Tez, now face to face with Colin. "I thought this being a grudge match and all, and I did call you out." He looked at Mark. "You too."

Colin laughed, his gang laughing with him.

"Really? And what you gonna wager?" "Same as we

agreed," said Tez.

Colin stopped laughing. Mark looked confused, but still amused by this new development.

"Done," said Colin, holding out a hand. Tez took it, shook it, tried to pull away. Colin held his hand tight, pulling the smaller man closer. "You know when I win," he whispered into Tez's ear, "her ass becomes mine."

Tez smiled. "You couldn't beat an old woman in a wheelchair."

"Well, we will see," said Colin, still holding his hand.

"So we doing this?" Tez asked.

Mark nodded, giving his brother a look.

"I'm calling you out," said Tez, loudly. "Both of you. If I win I get everything you have. I lose, you get all my stuff."

"Including her," Colin said, waving at Christie. She stuck her tongue out at him. "I like attitude," Colin leered back.

"Including her," said Tez.

Colin gave his hand a final shake, then let go, leaving red marks from his grip. Mark shook his hand a lot gentler and gave a sympathetic nod.

Everyone dispersed back to their rides, moving to line up either side of the first section, the drag race. The first car and bike raced, the race started by one person with a waved hand, the race decided by the four people at the finish line. Money was betted, won and lost as the races passed. Old Phipps made a considerable amount using his knowledge of racing. Christie watched nervously, still huddled in her jacket. Colin ignored the races, staring at her.

Finally the last drag race came. Tez lined the Volvo up on the spray painted line. Colin stopped next to him in his Skyline. Mark pulled up on the other side on his Kawasaki. The starter lined them up then stepped back.

With a drop of the hand the trio screamed forwards. The bike lifted the front wheel clear of the ground as Mark leant forwards to counter it. The Skyline spat smoke from all four wheels as the big engine tried to fire it forwards. The Volvo only spun the front wheels, but managed to edge partially ahead. By the finish line it was nearly a full bonnet ahead, Nissan and Kawasaki both dead level.

When the result came on the radio Christie gave a squeak of joy. Moans and jeers mixed with money as it was passed to winners. The three racers came back and parked where they were before. Mark laughed it off with his friends, shrugging and smiling. Colin shook off any offers of consolation and glared angrily at Tez.

The next set of races, the precision part, began, with both starting together on the miniature course marked only with spray paint markers. More was betted, risked and won. After the other grudges were settled the big three set up for their race. Colin was sweating in frustration, his short hair damp. Mark actually shook Tez by the hand before he put his gloves and helmet on.

Phipps made more bets, then stood beside Christie.

"This is going to be the fun bit, girlie," he said.

"Fun?" she asked, hair near dark with sweat.

"Yeah. That kid can drive, but this ain't made for three, you know what I mean?"

Christie looked at the narrow course and realised that two cars wouldn't fit, and it was even more impossible with the bike too.

"Be some body work to be done tonight," said Phipps, grunting and wandering off, still holding a wad of money in his hands.

Christie bit her lip and waited.

Tez shrugged his shoulders, trying to get comfortable in the shape hugging racing seat. The harness pinched, the warm weather made his back itch and the pressure to win was making him wish he could run away and piss in a hedge. Mark looked calm, sat on his bike, in the breeze. Colin just looked super mad, ready to explode. Tez hoped he would. He really, really hoped he would.

The starter lined them up, stood in his usual place, realised he would be run over there, shrugged, and stepped to the side. With a weak smile he dropped to the floor.

Mark held back, letting the cars battle on the narrow track while he kept out of it. Both the Volvo and the Nissan leapt forwards, wrestling for the lead. Colin knew how to set up a car, but Tez had the benefit of track set up and a lighter car, giving him a slight advantage. By the first corner, a few metres from the start, Tez had the inside and was ahead by a nose. Colin had to go wide to take the turn, forcing him to slow down. Tez flung the car around, hoping they didn't touch. Behind, the green H2R hung on his bumper, waiting. By the second corner Colin was on the inside, and on the offensive. They rubbed, knocking door mirrors in, as Colin bullied his way past. Tez was pushed out, braking hard and letting Mark past too. The next two corners brought them back to the main straight, and Tez flipped the power map switch on the dash, boosting the engine power and allowing him to pass both on the outside, cutting in hard for the end of straight corner. Colin resisted the urge to ram Tez from behind, instead he swung the car wide, aiming to carry the speed into the next bend and push past. Mark stayed back, close enough to take advantage, but safe from any aftermath.

Tez held the lead through the next lap, but Colin saw red and clipped his rear corner, sending him into a slide. With skills that surprised even Tez, he caught the slide, powered out, and managed to keep his place, pushing past the grey Skyline. Colin spat a curse at him, lost in the scream of racing engines and banging body panels. Tez smiled at Colin, planted the accelerator into the floor and pulled away.

Colin did push him from behind this time, sending him wide, but also letting Mark through. Canting the bike near horizontal Mark slid his knee on the floor as he took both cars on the inside. Colin screamed in rage and tried to clip the bike, but once out the corner it had the power to pull away. Tez got back on the track and soon caught up with Colin. With the car and bike ahead weaving Tez planned his moment carefully, let them both fall over each other, and squeezed past Colin on one bend, and took Mark on the inside of the next. Colin went to ram Tez but he swung back, hitting the front of the Skyline hard, making Colin ease off to keep control. Mark let Tez through, knowing to try and block could result in a nasty crash.

When they crossed the finish line Colin was alongside Mark again, and Tez was clear in the lead.

Tez didn't stop at the finish line. Instead he over ran, turned back hard and slid to a stop beside Christie. He leapt out and grabbed her, holding her tight. She hugged him back, kissing his damp cheek repeatedly. Mark stopped beside the Volvo, put down the side stand and hooked his helmet on the stubby mirror. When Tez looked back Mark nodded to him. Tez nodded back.

Colin screamed towards them, locking all four wheels and stopping with his front bumper touching the Volvo's rear. He threw the door open and stood.

Tez smiled at him, in front of everyone. Nobody else moved. They all wanted to see how it ended.

Colin looked at the floor as he walked slowly towards Tez.

"Looks like I won," said Tez.

"You wish," said Colin, stopping a few feet away and raising his head.

"I did. I was in front, remember? You must have seen it. I was in front of you after all." Tez smiled, Christie giggled.

Colin didn't smile.

"If you race fair, you wouldn't win," he said, menacing.

"Col, brother, he won," said Mark. Getting off his bike and offering a hand to Tez. Christie stepped back so the two men could shake.

"He didn't win," said Colin, not moving.

"You hate to lose, don't you?" asked Christie, taking a step towards him. "That's why you cheated at poker to get my dad in debt, that's why you race people you know you can beat. You can't stand knowing someone is better than you"

"Bull," grunted Colin, glaring at her.

"Yeah, right," she said. "That's why you let others take the crap for your stupid riot, why you blew up my home, and his garage, why you beat the crap out of me and my dad." "And you all deserved it. Bunch of pricks."

Tez smiled as Colin realised he'd admitted it. "Well, that changes the landscape a bit," he smiled.

Colin hesitated, then growled at Christie.

"Yeah, like the pathetic animal you are," she said. "You could never have me, or any other woman. Who wants to sleep with a dog, when they could have a real man."

Colin went slowly darker, shoulders hunched, fists clenched. Tez held a restraining hand to Christie but she shook him off.

"You tried to kill me, my dad, my man and his friends. You bastard. No wonder your family think you're the crap on their shoes, to be wiped off before you stink out their world. You bastard!" She screamed and spat at him. With lightning speed she slapped his face, making him rock back. As she turned to walk away there was a blur, and a loud bang. Christie looked shocked, and in disbelief. Red dripped from her back as she sank to her knees. Behind, Colin looked equally shocked, still holding the pistol. In the distant heat haze flashing blue lights followed the road towards them, sirens playing quietly, getting louder.

Christie looked with wet eyes to Tez. Phipps moved with surprising speed for an old man and floored Colin with one punch. Ricky and Tom sat on the stunned body while Tez cradled Christie in his arms.

"I'm sorry," she repeated. "I'm so, so sorry,"

"No, it was my fault," Tez tried to stop her speaking. "I did this."

The sirens grew louder as the line of patrol cars, riot vans, and an ambulance stopped. The paramedics took Christie into the ambulance, that sped off with two patrol cars escorting. Henderson parked his Range Rover by the Volvo and stopped to look over the scene. With a wave he sent three uniformed officers to arrest Colin, putting him in a patrol car and leaving after the ambulance. Henderson walked over to Tez, who was wiping his eyes and looking at the patch of red on the grey concrete.

"Well, kid. I guess it's over," Henderson said, looking at the stain.

"Yeah," Tez sniffed.

Henderson opened his mouth to speak, closed it and walked away. Mark stood beside Tez, and with remarkable tenderness put an arm around, giving him a man hug. Ricky and Tom helped the 4Mothion drivers and Yoki Riders peel the stickers off their cars and bikes. After a few minutes Tez pulled away from Mark, waved

Phipps away and got into the Volvo. Slowly he drove away, heading back to town.

In the Smelters Arms Tez sat in the snug, nursing a warm beer. Henderson came in and sat opposite him.

"Well," said Tez, looking up with a smile, "that worked."

"I didn't think it would," admitted Henderson, waving the barman over to order a drink.

"I had no doubt," said Tez, leaning back. "Hey! You took your time," he called to the figure that followed Henderson in.

"Sorry," said Christie. "Got a massive bruise on my back you git," she smiled, turned, and showed the purple bruise on her back.

"Yeah, should have told you really. They are called 'bullet proof vests' because they stop bullets, not bruises." Tez smiled as she playfully punched his shoulder. "Fake blood was a good effect, though."

Henderson nodded to them both. "Just come from the hospital with this one and heard on the radio that we have plenty now to lock up Colin, and finally close the books on this gang crap."

"Yeah, it's all mine now," smiled Tez.

"Almost a shame," said Henderson. "Gonna miss you lot, maybe."

"Miss us?" asked Christie.

"Yeah. New assignment, and a nice little promotion. Off to fight real crime now."

Tez raised his beer in mock salute. "Congratulations."

Henderson nodded and stood. Pausing he took his small whisky and swirled it. Raising it he said, "to you, and me. We didn't make a bad team."

Tez raised his beer, drank, then held out a hand. "Good

luck, Inspector Henderson."

"Chief Inspector Henderson," he corrected Tez, and smiled. "Thanks. Keep out of trouble." Henderson drained the whisky and set the glass down. "Behave," he said and left.

Christie waited for him to leave, then slapped Tez hard, and kissed him.

"What the hell?" he asked, rubbing his cheek.

"How did you know he was gonna shoot me in the back?" she hissed.

"I didn't, but he's a crazy person. They don't do much that's normal, hence the term 'crazy'."

Christie considered this, then slapped him again. "What if he shot me in the head?"

"I kinda hoped he wouldn't shoot you at all," said Tez.

"I hate you," she said with a smile. Tez leant closer and kissed her, softly. She bit his lip and held him close.

Alvin Thorpe was discharged into the care of his daughter the following week. He'd suffered serious injuries from the beating he'd been given by Colin, but was now well enough to live outside the hospital. With the insurance, and a large donation from Tez, the Black Bull was repaired and Tez was ordered by Alvin to move in. The car park was concreted over and became the regular meeting place for bikers, car enthusiasts and the locals. Christie was back behind the dark wood bar in short skirts getting long stares and big tips. Alvin resumed his poker nights with Maurice and Frederick, with Tez sitting in for some. Mick, Ricky and Tom all moved up to live in the Bull as well, while they rebuilt Hopdyke's garage, going into partnership together. Bicks had left, transferring with Henderson to help in his new assignment. On Saturday nights the car park was lined with a mix of bikes, cars and people all enjoying the company and the experience of the new scene.

Tez parked the Volvo by the picnic benches overlooking the town. Phipps was there in his old Land Rover, Mark had parked his bike next to it. Ricky and Tom parked behind the Volvo. Below the town bathed in the midsummer sun. They all stood in a line, looking down at the valley.

"Well, this is our town now," said Tez, feeling the words for the first time.

"Our town," repeated Mark.

"Yeah," said Ricky, looking at Phipps, who stared at Christie in her short shorts and bikini top.

"There were a few moments of doubt back there," said Tez.

"Which ones?" asked Ricky.

"All of them," Mark said.

They laughed, the sound a relief after the recent stress. Tez felt like a champion standing on a field of victory, a field he'd won.

Tez sighed. "All worked out in the end. We won, and nobody was hurt."

"Except me," said Christie, showing the dark bruise on her back.

"Except you, Babe."

"And me," said Phipps, rubbing his head.

"Be a bit quiet now," said Mark, to himself. "No more hassle."

"And a good thing," said Ricky.

"Maybe," said Mark.

"Sure we can find some new war to fight if you wanted, Mark," offered Christie. Mark just waved her away.

"I feel like another drink," Ricky said.

They all turned away, but Tez looked back.

"Home," he said.

BOOK TITLE

ABOUT THE AUTHOR

I am a massive reader who collects books. I love all genres but my favourite four authors are Stephen King, Michael Crichton, Terry Pratchett and Bernard Cornwall. Their influences show in my books and continues to form the backbone of my reading. My main area is sci-fi and techno thrillers so most of my work is in the future or the past.

I'm always writing, or thinking of writing even when I'm out and about. It does make conversations interesting when I ask the best way to kill someone! I hope you enjoy my books and please let me know what you think. The only thing better than writing a book is being told what it was like from others.

I live in the picturesque Midlands of England where there is scenery and action to inspire or relax the mind. I live with my wife, Deborah, my young son, Richard, a lot of books and a collection of strange cars.

Printed in Great Britain
by Amazon